Watermelon in a Cucumber Patch

Watermelon

in a

Cucumber
Patch

G. I. Shaw

Note: Books mentioned in text are real works and are referenced in the Bibliography at the end.

Published by
Joy Enterprises
332 S. Queen Street
Littlestown, PA 17340

Text Art by G. I. Shaw
Cover Art by Janette Toth
Composition by Kate Weisel
Printed by BookCrafters

Library of Congress Catalog Card Number: 93-81154
ISBN 0-9639450-0-9 (pbk)
Copyright © 1994 by G. I. Shaw

Manufactured in the United States of America
First Edition

March 1994

1 2 3 4 5 6 7 8 9 10

*Thanks to my parents
for all their support.
And to Darlene.*

Chapter One

 Stevi looked around the crowded locker room of Millpond High School. *Gym; the first day of school. What a bummer!* Her face burned as she struggled into her gym suit. "This must've shrunk," she muttered, shoving her glasses back up onto the bridge of her nose.

Her friend, Mona, giggled. Stevi sucked in her stomach, then gave the gym suit a mighty tug. Finally, it slid over her generous hips.

"You grew over the summer," said Mona, tossing her long blond hair. "*My* suit still fits." She laughed, then twirled on her toes like a ballerina.

"Your suit's tight at the bust and hips, too!" Stevi yanked her suit snaps together. They burst open again when she took a deep breath.

Mona's mouth turned down. Her blue eyes glittered. "At least I'm not popping out at the seams!" Slamming her locker door shut, she stomped out of the locker room with the rest of the girls' class.

Stevi blinked back tears. *When will I learn to keep my mouth shut?* Her stomach growled. She rummaged through her gym bag until she found a crumpled box of chocolate chip cookies, then stuffed one into her mouth. Gently, she shut the metal locker door.

Stevi stopped in the doorway to survey the gloomy gym. A fierce thunderstorm raged outside. Glass windows covered one wall. Usually, the football and baseball fields were visible, but today rain washed away the view. A loud clap of thunder made Stevi jump, and several girls in the gym squealed. The boys' class, which was sharing the gym, laughed.

Ari Toole's deep laugh drew Stevi's attention. Her heart raced. *Awesome,* she thought, admiring his exotic looks. *I wish he'd notice me.* Her shoulders slumped. *No . . . better that he doesn't, the way I look.*

Where's Mona? Stevi spotted her friend staring out the window, a hurt look on her face. Guilt flashed through Stevi. Slowly, she walked over to her friend. "I didn't mean to insult you, Mona." Stevi ran her fingers through her coffee-brown hair. "I'm just jealous of your figure."

Mona brushed a cookie crumb from Stevi's chin. "I guess we're both growing up . . . and out. Okay, you're forgiven." Her eyes twinkled mischievously as she tilted her head toward the boys. "Notice Ari?"

Stevi blushed and grinned.

Mrs. Nolan, the Phys. Ed. teacher, entered the gym briskly, blowing her whistle for attention. She looked ready for tennis in white shorts and T-shirt, her short graying hair pushed back in a no-nonsense style.

"Quiet, girls," said Mrs. Nolan. "Let's start with some warm-up exercises. Spread out so you don't hit your neighbor. Ready? Side-bends, everyone." Raising her arms over her head Mrs. Nolan bent to the side and bounced gently.

Stevi raised her arms. A thread popped . . . *Oh no! I'll die if my gym suit rips!*

Across the room the coach yelled, "Pay attention, boys!" The sound of laughter erupted. "To me, not the girls!"

Stevi could hear the boys' crude remarks.

"Look at the cute little blonde! Isn't she hot?"

Laughter . . . followed by, "What about the heifer next to her? Who wants odds her gym suit splits?"

Stevi's body was hot as if she had a sunburn. *Is he talking about me?* Another thread popped. Sweat beaded on her forehead. She wished she were invisible.

The coach blew his whistle, and the talking quieted; the boys began playing basketball. Sounds of heavy breathing, tennis shoes flapping on the floor and the whoosh of the basketball through the hoop filled the gym.

"Okay girls, toe-touch knee-bends," said Mrs. Nolan.

Stevi bent over to touch her toes, then squatted into a knee-bend. R-R-R-RIP. She gasped and straightened up, hiding her behind with her hands.

Her class roared with laughter. Across the room, the boys' game faltered. They gawked at the laughing girls.

"Mrs. Nolan, I-I have to r-return to the l-locker room," pleaded Stevi, backing from the gym.

Mrs. Nolan blew her whistle. Silence. "Stevi," she said, her words ringing across the gym, "I think you'd better plan on buying a bigger gym suit . . . today!"

A male voice slashed through the snickering. "What were those odds on that gym suit splitting?"

Stevi fled from the gym, tears racing down her cheeks. *I hate Phys. Ed., I hate school and I hate boys!* Slumped against her locker she sobbed as laughter rumbled from the gym.

An arm slipped around her shoulders. Stevi jumped. "It's okay, girl friend. We'll find a way to make it better," said Mona.

Stevi cried harder. "Go away! Nobody can help me. I'm fat and ugly and always will be!" She hung her head, wavy hair falling forward to cover her face.

"So you need to lose a few pounds, Stevi. We'll just put you on a diet." Mona started undressing.

Stevi removed her glasses. "Dieting doesn't work for me." She scrubbed tears from her eyes, smearing mascara across her face. "What are you doing in here? You'll get in trouble for ditching gym class." She peeled the torn gym suit from her body.

Mona patted Stevi on the back. "What's more important, Phys. Ed. or friendship?" She ripped the towel from her locker, then headed for the showers.

Stevi grabbed her towel, wrapped it around her—tugging to make it meet. "Thanks, Mona. I don't know what I'd do without you. You're the only person I can talk to."

Mona turned on the hot shower. "It's time to stop talking and find out how to help you."

"Is there really any help for me?" Stevi slipped under the hot spray. Her tension flowed down the drain with the hot water.

"I bet the library has a section on weight control," said Mona, patting herself dry. "Let's meet at the bus stop after school and I'll help you look."

Stevi brushed water from her eyes. Shrugging, she said, "I don't know what good it will do, but I guess it's worth a try."

"Come on, girl friend, let's get dressed," said Mona.

Chapter Two

After school, Stevi raced home. She tossed her books on the breakfast bar in the kitchen. Snatching a bag of potato chips from the snack shelf, she sprinted out the back door. The day was still dreary, although the rain had stopped. She strolled to the bus stop where she and Mona often met under an ancient oak tree.

Water dripped from the branches of the tree onto a concrete bus stop bench. Stevi paced back and forth, nibbling chips. *What am I doing here? I've tried losing weight before. Besides . . . who cares if I'm fat? I don't have a boyfriend; I can't date until I'm sixteen. IT'S JUST NOT FAIR! Everyone else can eat anything they want and not get fat. I'm the only one who gains weight!* Anger burned Stevi's throat. She crushed the empty potato chip bag and flung it into a trash can.

A bus lumbered to a stop, and Mona jumped off. Tight jeans

hugged her body. Her expensive red sweater stretched across her full breasts when she turned to wave good-bye to a boy on the bus.

Jealousy stabbed Stevi's heart; she clenched her teeth. Thunder echoed in the distance while heavy gray clouds rolled across the horizon. She scrutinized the sky. *That's how I feel.* Gruffly, she said, "Should we walk to the library, or catch the next bus?"

"I asked Jake to pick us up," said Mona, checking the time on the three watches she wore on her left wrist. "Isn't he to die for?" She giggled. "I just love his bronze-colored hair!"

Stevi cleaned her glasses on the corner of her pink great-shirt. "I can't ride in cars with boys. You know that." Holding her glasses to the light, she frowned. "Mom will ground me if she finds out."

"Your mom's at work. How will she know?"

Stevi shrugged.

Jake's '87 sea-foam green Chevy screeched to a halt, scraping the tires on the curb. The door swung open, and a tall black-haired boy got out. "Hey dudes, hop in," he said.

Stevi's heart pounded like a jackhammer.

Mona sashayed toward the car, hips and hair swinging in opposite directions. "Hi ya, Ari. I'll sit up front with Jake."

Ari glared at Stevi. "You coming, doll face?"

Stevi's mind raced. *Mom's at work . . . how will she know?* The rules flew from her head. "Okay, sure!"

Ari shoved the seat forward, then stepped back against the car door. Stevi's shirt caught on a sharp edge of the door. Yanking it free, she backed into Ari. "S-sorry," she muttered, feeling her face flame. She struggled the rest of the way into the car.

Ari crawled in after her. Their gazes locked. Stevi's insides turned to jelly staring into Ari's almond-shaped eyes. *If ever I needed a reason to lose weight, this is it!*

Ari smiled, brushing shiny black hair from his face. Kindness twinkled in his black eyes. "Didn't tear your shirt, did you?" His voice sounded like a kettledrum, deep and smooth. Chills ran up Stevi's back. She tried to speak and couldn't, so she shook her head.

Jake put the car in gear. "Where to?"

"Stevi needs to go to the library," said Mona. She snuggled up to Jake. "What's happening, dudes?"

"Basketball tryouts at school," said Jake, wrenching the car into traffic, tires squealing.

"I bet he spends a fortune on tires," Stevi mumbled.

Ari leaned close to Stevi. "You say something?"

Her nose twitched. The smell of damp denim and stale cigarette smoke floated from Ari's ragged jacket. "Just that we're supposed to go to the library," she whispered. *If he asks me why, I'll die.*
Please don't let Mona say anything. She scrunched into her seat hoping Ari couldn't hear her pounding heart.

Jake's jade-green eyes peered at Stevi in the rearview mirror.
"You girls want to watch us try out for the team?"

Mona bounced to her knees. "Awesome! I'd love to!"

Jake reached into his jacket pocket pulling out a pack of ciga-
rettes. He stuck one in his mouth, then offered one to Mona.

Self-righteously, she shook her head. "They cause wrinkles."

Ari reached for a cigarette, but Stevi interrupted. "Smoking's
not good for athletes," she said.

"Besides," said Mona, tilting her head saucily, "they make
your breath smell bad." She gave Jake a knowing wink.

Ari put the cigarette back. Disgusted, Jake shook his head,
took a long drag, then tossed the cigarette out the window.

With one clammy hand, Stevi dug a roll of hard candy out of
her jeans' pocket. "I really do need to go to the library," she said,
offering the roll to Ari. She popped a piece into her mouth, com-
forted by its sweetness.

"Chill out," said Jake. "I'll drop you at the library."

"I'm going with you guys," said Mona. "We'll come back for
you in a couple of hours. Okay, Stevi?"

Stevi nodded. *Ari must think I'm a geek. But I can't take a*
chance on being seen running around in this car. If Mom finds out,
I'm dead.

The car screeched to a halt in the library parking lot. Stevi
squeezed past Ari.

"Bummer, doll face. Wish you were going with us," he said.

Stevi trembled. *If he only knew how much I want to go.*

Mona waved. "Later, dude."

Ari waved from the back window as the car careened around
the corner.

As if sensing Stevi's feelings, thunder crashed around her.
Lightning rippled through the dark layers of clouds like a light show.
Cold rain slashed down, drenching her.

Stevi dashed for the door. "My luck! First I turn down a chance
to be with Ari; now I get drenched. I wish I were more like Mona."

The library was empty except for three librarians and one old man reading at one of the worktables. She was glad no one else was there. Stevi pushed wet hair away from her face, then crossed the room to the computer catalog. The librarian at the main desk frowned at the trail of footprint-shaped puddles on the floor.

Stevi searched the catalog for diet books. The main group was in the 613 range. She scanned the numbers at the end of the shelves until she found the right one. *Golly! There must be fifty books on weight control. How will I ever decide?* She wished Mona were here.

Confused, Stevi pulled several books from the shelf without regard to their titles. She headed toward the nearest worktable. Rounding the corner, she bumped into two of her classmates.

She froze . . . her mouth open. *They'll tell everyone about seeing me with diet books. I'll be the school joke. What am I going to say?*

Chapter Three

Carin's ice-blue stare swept over Stevi. "Want to join us? We're waiting for the gang to finish basketball tryouts."

Hugging the diet books to her chest, Stevi shook her head. "I'm working on a report that's due tomorrow," she said, guilty about the lie.

Terrina's black corn-row braids quivered like snakes, as she laughed. "Stevi . . . always the bookworm. Don't study too hard."

"Bummer," said Carin. "Come on over if you get done." She and Terrina sauntered toward the magazine racks in the middle of the library. Watching her classmates' thin bodies, envy filled Stevi. Carin, short with creamy-colored curls, was a sharp contrast to Terrina's tall, lanky black image. Stevi's confidence wavered. *Maybe I should walk home. Nobody will miss me.*

The library door slammed open. "Oops, I did it again," said Jesse Means, the tallest and strongest boy in Stevi's class. He reminded her of Arnold Schwarzenegger. "Sorry, Ms. Librarian, I didn't mean to break your door!" Jesse laughed.

Brian Steinberg followed Jesse into the library. He was as quiet as Jesse was loud. Short and stocky, Brian never stood out in a crowd. He dated Carin and most of the kids, including Stevi, wondered what pretty Carin saw in him. Today he was smiling, and Stevi thought he was almost handsome.

It's getting crowded in here! Stevi scurried to the circulation desk and plopped her books down. The librarian scanned Stevi's library card, then the back of her books. Their titles appeared on the computer screen as if by magic. The librarian asked, "Having a weight problem?"

Stevi cringed, hoping no one would hear. "Doing a project for school."

The librarian pushed the books across the counter. "Have a nice day." She turned away.

Stevi clutched the books. Twirling toward the door, she tripped over Ari. Books flew from her arms scattering like autumn leaves. She gasped, then her eyes widened. "Where'd you come from?" Mortified, she dropped to her knees.

"Let me help you," said Ari, also bending. Their heads crashed together knocking them off their feet. Stevi recoiled, slammed into the circulation desk, then slid down onto the floor. Momentarily, the room darkened around her. As the ringing in her ears faded, she heard Ari's voice. "Are you all right?"

"I-I think so. How about you?"

Chuckling, Mona and Jake surveyed the sprawling mess.

Ari gathered Stevi into his arms, helping her to her feet. Her skin tingled where he touched her. "Thank you, Ari."

He started to pick up the library books. Her face crimson, Stevi screamed, "NO! I'll get them."

Ari looked confused. "Just trying to help." He handed the books to Stevi.

She hid them behind her great-shirt. Seeing her other classmates approaching, she changed the subject. "Did you and Jake make the basketball team?"

"Of course," said Jake, grinning smugly. "The team couldn't survive without us."

"Talk about conceit," said Mona. She snuggled into Jake's arms. "Let's go to the Burger 'n' Bun for burgers."

"I'm always ready to eat," said Jesse. The rest of the teenagers agreed.

"I have to get home," said Stevi. "My mom will be home from work in a few minutes, and I have to catch the next bus."

"We'll give you a ride," said Jake.

Ari reached for Stevi's books. "Let me carry those for you."

Panic. "No thanks. I've got them." A warm feeling spread from Stevi's heart. *He likes me in spite of my making a fool of myself.* "Jake, will you drop me off at the end of my block? My parents don't like me riding in cars, yet."

"Stevi's parents are strict," said Mona.

"No problem," said Jake. He waved to the rest of the gang. "We'll meet you at the Burger 'n' Bun in a few minutes."

In the back seat of Jake's Chevy, Stevi kept glancing at Ari. *He's so good looking. I wonder if he really likes me?*

Mona kept up a constant chatter in the front seat. She said, "Stevi, you and Ari should go out sometime."

Stevi wanted to crawl into a hole and pull it in after her. She peeked at Ari from the corner of her eye. His face was pink, too. Their glances met, then repelled. *I'll never hear from him again.* It was a quiet ride home.

Saturday, Stevi lounged on her purple bedspread in her bedroom while eating a peanut butter sandwich and flipping through her library books.

A bookshelf filled with glass horses stood against one pale pink wall. Stevi's desk, cluttered with books and papers, sat under the side window. Horse posters competed with rock stars for space around the walls. Two walk-in closets lined the wall opposite the bed with a blond chest of drawers standing between the doors. A matching dresser sat next to the entrance door.

Mom yelled up the stairs, "Stevi, come down and help with the yard work."

"I can't, Mom, I'm studying."

"Get down here this minute, or I'm coming up to get you!" Mom sounded angry.

"All right already," said Stevi, slamming *Dr. Atkins' New Diet Revolution* shut. *I'm not ready to diet anyway!* She stomped downstairs, then out the back door letting it slam behind her.

Mom shoved a rake into Stevi's hand. "Start raking. It's time you did your share of the work around here."

Stevi grumbled under her breath. "A person can't get any time to herself." She raked in silence for a while.

The fenced yard surrounded aged oak trees towering over the Cape Cod house. The tiny front yard dropped sharply onto a steep hill covered with ivy. Concrete steps climbed from the sidewalk to the yard, then to a porch on the front of the house.

"Mom, what would you say if I wanted to go on a diet?"

Mom leaned her chubby figure on her rake studying Stevi. "You could stand to lose a few pounds, but you're not that bad. What brought this on?"

Stevi kept her eyes trained on the ground. "You know I had to buy a new gym suit. I've been looking through a few diet books and thought I might try to lose some weight."

Frowning, Mom stuffed leaves into an orange pumpkin trash bag. "Now might not be a good time to start a diet, Stevi. Diets usually require special menus and we can't afford it right now. I'm working fewer hours, and your dad's company is laying off people. Maybe you wouldn't be so heavy if you stopped eating between meals."

Stevi's shoulders drooped. "Right." She jabbed at the leaves with her rake. "Blame everything on me."

Chapter Four

Sunday, after church, Stevi set the dining-room table with the good china. Sun streamed through the picture window at the end of the room making the dishes sparkle. She removed the good set of glasses from the china cabinet placing them on the table. Her ten-year-old brother burst into the room waving her diet books over his head.

"Look what I found in Fatty's room," Nick said, dancing around the table. "She's trying to lose weight," he gasped, laughing. "What a lost cause!"

"What were you doing in my room, Creep?" Stevi screeched.

Nick, small and quick, raced around the table taunting her. "Fatty, fatty, two-by-four, can't get through the kitchen door!"

"Mom," Stevi wailed. "Make him give my books back." Her eyes flashed in anger and her mouth twisted into an ugly grin as she whispered, "I'll get you, Twerp."

"Stop, this instant," Mom bellowed from the kitchen. "Nick,

give back the books. Stevi, apologize for calling your brother names."

"Why should I apologize? He started it!" Hands on her hips, Stevi defiantly stared into her mother's dark eyes, so like her own.

"Don't speak to me in that tone of voice, young lady." Mom brushed a strand of graying hair from her face. A streak of spaghetti sauce was left on her forehead.

"Mom," Stevi whined. "It's not fair. Nick gets away with everything."

"Another word, and you'll be grounded."

When Mom turned back to her cooking, Nick stuck his tongue out at Stevi. He mouthed the words, "Fatty, fatty, two-by-four . . ." but didn't say them aloud.

Stevi snarled, "You geek . . ."

"Stevi," Mom snapped. "Go to your room! You're grounded for a week."

Stevi stomped upstairs. *I'll get even!* She slammed her bedroom door. *It's not fair grounding me and not Nick.* She heaved the library books across the room, then slumped into her desk chair.

Yanking open the bottom desk drawer she found a cupcake she'd hidden earlier and stuffed it into her mouth. Her mind churned. *Just because he's the baby he can get away with anything.* She reached for another snack cake, then stopped in midair, grimacing. *Why am I doing this to myself? What's wrong with me? No wonder I'm a blimp.* She rested her head on her arms and sobbed.

Later that week, Stevi and Mona were hurrying to math class. "You're grounded again?" Mona clutched Stevi's arm. "What a bummer!"

"Yeah . . . well, you know my parents," said Stevi. Her voice was flat, and her shoulders sagged. "I don't care. Nobody cares."

Mona looked perplexed, then smiled impishly. "Let's ditch school Friday and go to the mall."

"I don't know. . . . I'm already in enough trouble."

"We'll make it a party and invite the gang." Mona's eyes glittered. "We can go to the movies and shopping, then pig-out on pizza."

Stevi shrugged. "I can't afford it. The situation isn't so good at home."

She and Mona settled into their desks. The math teacher entered the room. Mona leaned over and whispered, "Maybe you should look for a job?"

Visions of new clothes, CDs and being independent filled Stevi's head. Her eyes twinkled. "I'll get back to you about Friday." She was grinning when the math teacher put an end to their conversation.

That evening, Stevi sat at the dinner table staring out the window behind Dad's chair. Dad had on jeans and a T-shirt rather than his usual suit. Nick played with the liver on his plate. When he thought no one was watching, he slipped bites to the cat sitting on his lap.

When everyone finished eating, Dad said, "We need to talk."

Mom stacked the dinner plates, then brought slices of chocolate cake for dessert.

"I was laid off today," Dad said, looking sad. He ran his hand across his balding scalp. "We're going to have to work together as a family to get through this crisis."

Fear made Stevi's hands and feet cold. "What will we do, Dad?"

Nick turned away. Tears sneaked down his cheeks.

"Don't worry, Honey," said Mom, her face pale. "Everything will be okay." She gave Nick a hug.

"You can keep my allowance," said Nick.

Mom and Dad smiled. "Thanks, Big Guy," said Dad. "We'll be all right. Why don't you go watch TV?"

"Mom. Dad. What do you think about me getting a part-time job?" Stevi looked anxiously from one to the other.

"Mother?" One of Dad's eyebrows arched like it always did when he asked Mom's opinion. "Is she ready for a job yet?"

Mom stared at Stevi, thoughtfully. "You'll be sixteen next week. Can you handle school, homework, your chores *and* a job?"

Stevi drew designs in a smear of cake icing with her fork. "If I had a job, I could help with the bills. You wouldn't need to give me an allowance." She studied her parents' faces. "If my grades drop, I'll quit." Acid burned in her stomach.

"Okay, I suppose you can give it a try," said Mom.

Dad pushed his empty plate away. Grinning, he picked up the newspaper and opened it to the classified ads. "I'd better check out the good jobs, before you get there first."

Nick flew back into the room. "No one will hire her," he said. "She's too fat and dumb."

"Watch your mouth, Creep," Stevi snarled.

Mom's eyes narrowed. "You'd better start acting your age if you want people to think you're responsible enough to have a job."

Stevi trembled and bit her lip to keep from shouting. *I'll show them! I'll ditch school Friday and go to the mall. We'll just see who's too fat and dumb to get a job!*

Chapter Five

Clammy fog shrouded Friday morning like soggy cereal. Stevi shivered in the cold, then pulled her raincoat tighter around her. Ghostly shadows loomed around the bus stop. Unable to discern who was there, Stevi realized no one could see her either.

Like a shadow, she glided toward her classmates. Mona's voice cut through the gloom. "Stevi and I are going to the mall. Who wants to go?"

"How will we get there?" Terrina gestured at the sky. "This sure isn't the kind of day to walk."

"Jake is picking me up in a while," said Brian. He huddled further into his school jacket. "He's *always* ready to ditch school. I bet he'll drive us."

"Morning, Stevi," said Mona, spying her friend.

Suddenly, Jake's Chevy materialized in the murkiness. Brian bounded to the car, then spoke briefly with Jake, and Ari who was with him. Turning, Brian motioned the group to come on. They piled into the car.

The fog was lifting as the car pulled into the nearly empty mall parking lot. The teens abandoned the car, tossing coats and rain gear into the trunk. Jake tickled Mona. She squealed. The group laughed and frolicked, in high spirits.

Ari tried the mall door, checked his watch, then said, "Drat! We're too early. The mall's not open yet."

"Gnarly," said Terrina. "What'll we do?"

"Let's make some plans," said Mona, hopping onto a low brick wall near the mall door. She sat, her legs swinging, and said, "Let's go to a movie. They're cheaper in the morning." She giggled. "We can sneak from one cinema to the other."

"Yeah," said Ari. "Maybe we can see all four movies for the price of one!"

"I'm going to look for a job," said Stevi, softly.

Mona twirled toward Stevi. "No way! Ditching school should be fun."

Stevi shrugged. "I need the money."

"I'll treat," said Mona. "I'll treat everyone."

Ari scowled. "We've got money." Offended, his face hardened.

"Chauvinist!" Mona, hands on her hips, stared into Ari's face. "I have more money than the rest of you. I'll pay for the first ticket. Then we'll see who can sneak into the most movies for free. If you get caught, you're on your own."

Sensing a battle of wills, Stevi changed the subject. "I *really* do need to look for a job. You go to the movies, and I'll meet you later."

"Nerd!" said Mona.

"Mona?" Stunned, Stevi shoved her glasses back on her nose.

"You *never* want to have any fun!" said Mona. Hair swinging, she marched to the mall door and yanked. "It's open," she said, disappearing inside. Terrina and Brian followed her.

Ari grabbed Stevi's arm. "Are you sure about this? I was looking forward to spending the day with you."

Stevi hung her head, then nodded. "I have to get a job." She stared into his sexy eyes. Her heart threatened to explode. She whispered, "I don't have a choice." Her eyes pleaded with him: *Don't ask why.*

Ari searched her face, then shrugged. "Okay. Later, dude." He ran to catch Jake and Brian.

Stevi surveyed the mall, undecided where to start. Mentally she eliminated Jerri's Beauty Bazaar. She had no interest or training in styling hair. In fact, she had no training at all. You wouldn't catch her dead in Big Girls Are Us! Cuddly Pets was out because cleaning up after animals wasn't her idea of fun either.

Finally gathering her courage, she marched into Surrell's Department store. *A store this big should have something I can do.*

"Excuse me," said Stevi, to a saleslady straightening dresses in the Junior Shop. "Who do I see about getting a job?"

The lady studied Stevi's baggy blouse, tight jeans and scruffy tennis shoes. A disapproving look crossed her face. "We're not hiring," she said, in a haughty voice. "Haven't you heard the economy's bad?" She turned her back, muttering, "Teenagers! How do they expect to get jobs looking like ragamuffins?"

Drooping, Stevi whispered, "Thanks anyway," then tramped out. *Now I know why Dad was so sad last night. Asking for a job is humiliating.*

Courage gone, Stevi shuffled through the mall. A small "Help Wanted" sign in Awesome Rags Teen Shop caught her eye. She squared her shoulders. *I can get this job.*

A tiny lady greeted Stevi as she entered the store. "How may I help you?"

She sounds so cheerful. This must be a great place to work. "I'd like to apply for the job," Stevi said, motioning toward the "Help Wanted" sign.

The saleslady pointed toward the back of the store. "Speak to Mrs. Laird. She's the lady with curly brown hair standing near the cash register."

"Thanks." Stevi's hands were cold and clammy. She rubbed them together. *All they can do is say no,* she thought, striding purposefully through the store.

The cashier and manager talked, and hung skirts from a gigantic box. The manager, Mrs. Laird, was slightly taller than Stevi. "Excuse me," said Stevi. "I'd like to apply for the job."

When she turned toward Stevi, Mrs. Laird's eyes were hidden behind tortoiseshell-framed glasses. Her smile brittle, she asked, "Are you sixteen?"

"I will be next week."

"Lucy, give the young lady an application." To Stevi, she said, "I'll interview you after you fill it out." She returned to hanging skirts.

The cashier handed the application to Stevi. "Do you need a pen?" Stevi shook her head, then glanced around for some place to sit. Lucy said, "Fill it out on the end of the counter."

Leaning on the counter, Stevi studied the application. The first part was easy; name, address, the usual. The rest was harder. She didn't have any work references, and she had no idea who to put down for personal ones. Finally, she wrote down Mona's name and that of her Sunday School teacher. Her hands shook as she handed the application to Mrs. Laird.

Mrs. Laird gave the application a cursory glance. "No experience? What hours are you available?"

Hope surged through Stevi. Trembling, she said, "Evenings and weekends, I guess." She held her breath.

Mrs. Laird said, "I'm still taking applications. I'll call you and let you know." Tossing the application behind the counter, she turned back to her work.

Deflated, Stevi's body sagged. "Thanks," she mumbled, then slipped from the store.

Suddenly, she was ravishingly hungry. The Yogurt Palace stood across the mall. *Yogurt is good for me.* She ordered a double cup with honey and nuts.

Sitting on a bench in the middle of the mall, she savored each soothing bite. She glanced up. A "Help Wanted" sign was hanging on the door of Butterball Bakery. *It might be fun working in a bakery! I'll try it.* When she finished eating she was calm.

She pulled a mirror from her purse, applied lipstick, then ran a comb through her hair to bolster her courage. *I WILL get this job,* she thought, then marched toward the bakery.

Chapter Six

A tiny bell tinkled when Stevi opened the door to the Butterball Bakery. The smell of freshly baked bread washed over her. As the door closed the bell tinkled again. She hesitated, breathing in the wonderful aroma.

A huge, red-haired woman lumbered from the back room of the bakery. She wore a turquoise smock as bright as her curly carrot-colored hair. Large crooked teeth filled her smile. "Morning, dearie," she said. Her voice was loud but sweet. "What can I get you?"

Stevi smiled in response. "Hi! I'd like to apply for a job."

The woman's smile widened. "The job's for two nights a week, dearie, every Saturday and a half day every third Sunday. Had any experience?"

Stevi's shoulders slumped. "No. I've never had a job before, but I learn quickly, and the hours would be fine."

Stevi didn't think the woman's smile could get wider, but it did. Her cheeks were like red golf balls. Her eyes disappeared in crinkles of fat. "Name's Rosie. Come to my office and fill out an application. If you can make change, the job's yours."

Flooded with happiness, Stevi followed Rosie to the office. She filled out an application while Rosie went back to work. She took the completed application out front as Rosie finished waiting on a customer. Rosie thrust out her fat hand. "Let's see what we have here." She studied the application.

"Well, Stevi dear, I see you'll be sixteen next Wednesday. Can you start work the following Monday?"

Stevi beamed and nodded.

"Be here at six P.M. Don't be late. I can't stand tardiness. I'll train you from six until nine the next three evenings; Saturday, too. The following week you'll start your regular shift of Tuesday and Thursday nights. When I'm sure you know your stuff, I'll put you on the Sunday schedule. You work alone on Sundays, but a healthy-looking girl like you shouldn't have any problems. Okay, dearie?"

"Awesome! *Thanks,* Rosie. You won't be sorry." Stevi dashed from the bakery. Outside, she jumped for joy. *YES! I GOT A JOB! I GOT A JOB!* She spun like a top, and wanted to shout it to the whole world. *I've got to tell Mona . . . and my parents . . . AND NICK.* She grinned smugly.

She skipped down the mall, searching for her friends, the interview racing through her mind. Suddenly, she stopped as if welded to the spot. *A "healthy-looking" girl like me? What did Rosie mean?* Her mouth dropped open. *I got the job because I'm FAT! Rosie thinks I'll be a good advertisement for the bakery.*

Shame, despair, then anger rippled through Stevi. She shuffled, like an old woman, to the nearest mall bench where she sat hunched over, eyes unfocused and glassy. She brooded on whether to take the job or forget the whole idea.

Some time later, Terrina's loud voice penetrated her gloom. "That was awesome, dudes. I could sit through that movie again."

"You think everything is awesome," said Brian.

Ari's deep laugh vibrated. "You jealous?"

"There's Stevi," said Mona. "Hey, Stevi, did you get a job?"

Stevi tried to smile. "Yeah, sure did."

Ari's black eyes glittered. "Awesome, dude! Where and when do you start working?"

Stevi's face flamed. She mumbled, "I start a week from Monday, at the Butterball Bakery."

"I'm hungry," said Jake. "Let's go to the Pizza Crib."

"My treat," said Mona.

Ari growled, "I can pay my own way." He stood, feet apart, hands on hips, as if ready to do battle.

"I got it." Mona waved a wad of bills in the air. "I copped the grocery money from my mom before she got up this morning. I'll treat—to celebrate Stevi's job."

Ari shrugged.

"Won't you get into trouble?" Stevi pushed her glasses up on her nose.

"Don't worry, girl friend. I'll tell Dad I needed the money for clothes." Mona strutted toward the Pizza Crib. "We got plenty of money. We're rich."

Ari stuck his nose in the air and mimicked Mona behind her back. Everyone but Stevi laughed.

In the Pizza Crib, Mona ordered three large pies, all with different toppings. The young people pulled two tables together.

"Shame we can't order a beer," said Jake. "Then we could really party."

"You want a *real* party, try crack," said Mona.

Shocked, Stevi gasped. *Mona must be kidding.*

"Right," said Terrina. "Like you know where to get it."

Mona smirked. "One of our friends is dealing, Ms. Know-It-All." Just then, the waitress brought the pizza. They all dived into the food.

Stevi listened to the easy banter between friends, but stayed out of the conversation. She finished a fourth slice of pizza, and reached for the last slice when Jake did.

Jake snapped, "How about leaving some for the rest of us?"

Face burning, Stevi yanked her hand back as if she'd touched a snake. "Sorry," she mumbled. *What a pig I am!*

"I thought girls were picky eaters," said Brian. Everyone laughed, except Stevi.

Wishing she could die, she said through stiff lips, "I've got to go. It's late and my mom will be off work soon. Thanks for the pizza, Mona." She shoved her chair back so hard, it toppled. She righted it, then shoved it under the table.

I've got to get out of here! She ran for the door. Laughter followed her. She glanced back. *I hate it when they laugh at me.* The Pizza Crib door opened. Stevi collided with the person entering.

She stepped back, and said, "Excuse me . . ."

It was her mother. "Stevi? What are you doing here? Why aren't you in school?"

Oh no! Stevi froze. *Please, not in front of my friends.*

Chapter Seven

Mom's dark eyes blazed. She grabbed Stevi by the arm, yanking her back inside the Pizza Crib. She demanded again, "Why aren't you in school?"

Stevi looked frantically from Mom to her friends. They were watching. Tears flooded her eyes. "Mom, *please,* can we go outside?" Her stomach churned. She was afraid the pizza would come back up.

"No, young lady! Explain yourself this instant!"

"Mom, you're causing a scene. Can we at least sit down and talk quietly?"

Lips clenched, Mom ran a hand through her short hair. She noticed everyone staring. "The car's outside," she said, in a low menacing voice. "Get in. I'll be right out." In her anger, she shoved Stevi through the door.

Stevi stumbled out to the car, dizzy with relief. Hopping in, she said a silent prayer for the words to explain. By tomorrow, the story would be all over school. She wished she could curl into a tiny ball and roll away. Tears slipped down her cheeks, fogging her glasses.

Mom jerked open the car door, shoving a pizza box at Stevi. She slid behind the steering wheel. "Start talking."

"I-I took the day off to look for a job." Stevi peeked at Mom's face, hard from controlled anger. Stevi continued. "I got a job at Butterball Bakery, starting a week from Monday." Mom's face didn't soften. "Will you let me keep it?"

"Cutting school isn't the type of behavior I expected from someone old enough to work," said Mom. "We'll discuss this with your father."

Stevi trembled. "Please Mom. You said I could get a job. I *had* to go during the day, or I might not have gotten hired. I'll make up what I missed in school, I promise. If my grades drop, I'll give up the job. I want to help with the family's expenses."

Mom glared at Stevi. "All right, you can keep the job. But you're grounded until it starts and that includes your birthday."

After a few moments, Stevi said, "Thanks. . . . Mom? Do we have to tell Dad?"

Frowning, Mom said, "I guess not. He has enough worries."

Stevi leaned her head back on the seat and closed her eyes. She sagged, drained of emotion. *Thank you, God,* she prayed.

On Monday, Mona bounded into the school cafeteria, then plopped her lunch on the table next to Stevi. "Why wouldn't your Mom let me talk to you Sunday?"

"Except for Red Cross class, I'm grounded again, including my birthday."

Mona shook her head in disbelief. "Bummer! What about your job?"

"I can keep it, *if* I keep my grades up." She unwrapped a fruit pie, broke it in half, offering some to Mona. Mona shook her head. Stevi gobbled it in two bites.

Mona poked at the remains of Stevi's lunch. "I thought you were dieting."

"I want to, but I can't get motivated." Stevi sighed. "I've been reading diet books. I've asked Mom to pack a light lunch but she's still packing pie and cookies and potato chips."

Mona shuddered. "Ugh! Fat, sugar and calories. What books have you read?"

"I've read *Dr. Atkins' New Diet Revolution,* about eating low carbohydrates; *Thin So Fast,* about liquid protein diets; and *The Deadly Diet: Recovering from Anorexia and Bulimia.* That's about taking laxatives and vomiting. Sounds terrible and it's dangerous. I started to read *Feeding the Empty Heart* but it was about people who have alcoholics as parents. My parents don't drink so I didn't think it applied to me."

Mona looked puzzled. "You couldn't find anything to help?"

"Well, I saw a book called *The Woman Doctor's Diet for Teen-Age Girls,* but someone else had it checked out when I went back." Frustrated, Stevi said, "I even paged through a book called *Don't Diet.* I just don't know what to read or believe."

Mona rested her head in her hands, staring into space, thinking. "Have you tried exercise?"

Stevi shuddered. "I *hate* exercise. I do enough in gym class."

"Maybe not," said Mona. "Let's get together and jog."

Stevi made a face and shook her head.

"Walk, then," said Mona.

"You forget, I'm grounded."

"I'm sure if you explained, your mom would let you walk."

Stevi smiled sadly. "I wouldn't count on it. She's pretty mad at me right now."

"Call and ask. All she can do is say no." Mona put her arm around Stevi. "Do you want me to talk to her for you?"

"Would you?"

"Sure, what are friends for?"

Later that day, Mona grabbed Stevi as she was getting her math book from her locker. "I called your mom. You're right. She's really angry."

Stevi nodded. "I warned you."

"I had the idea that maybe we could walk in the mall next week when you start work," said Mona.

"I'll see if I can get out of the house early."

Jake walked up, then slipped his arm around Mona. "Ready?"

"Yeah. See ya, Stevi."

Forlornly, Stevi watched Mona and Jake exchange a kiss. *Will I ever have a boy friend?*

* * *

At six o'clock sharp on the following Monday evening, the tinkling bell announced Stevi's arrival at Butterball Bakery. Stevi bounced in, calling, "Evening, Rosie. I'm ready to work."

Rosie waddled around the counter, and threw a heavy arm across Stevi's shoulders. "Let's go into the office and get you a hairnet, dearie."

Stevi stuffed her hair into the net, then grimaced at her reflection in the mirror. She looked like something out of a 1930's movie. She hoped none of her friends saw her like this.

Learning the computerized cash register wasn't easy. Stevi concentrated hard, but constantly needed to refer to the thick instruction manual, kept under the counter.

"Time for a break," said Rosie. Surprised, Stevi looked up. "You get fifteen minutes weekday evenings, and thirty minutes on Saturdays for lunch."

"Will my breaks be the same time? My friend, Mona, wants to come walk around the mall with me for exercise."

"Depends on who you're working with, dearie. The person with seniority gets to pick the break time."

"Is it all right to call my friend?"

"No personal calls, *or visits* allowed from friends, unless they're customers. I'm paying you to work, dearie, not goof off."

What a bummer. Stevi gritted her teeth. *Rosie was so sweet before I started working. Now she sounds like my mother.* "May I go into the mall on my break?"

"What you do on your break is your business, dearie, as long as you get back on time." The bell announced a customer.

Stevi grabbed her purse and ran out of the bakery. She scrounged through her wallet for a quarter to call Mona from a pay phone.

The phone rang and rang. At last Mrs. Webb sleepily answered. "Not here," she replied to Stevi. "Went out with some guy hours ago."

"Drat!" Stevi slammed the phone onto its receiver, then checked her watch. She still had ten minutes of her break to go window-shopping. Strolling through the mall, she daydreamed of the beautiful clothes she would buy when she lost weight. *Then Ari will find me attractive and ask me out.*

She glanced at her watch. PANIC! She'd been daydreaming for twenty minutes. Heart pounding, she raced for the bakery.

Chapter Eight

Gasping for breath, Stevi slammed through the bakery door and into a departing customer. Stevi's glasses flew from her face, bounced off the customer's pastry box and onto the floor. The pastry box slid from the customer's hands, hit the floor and burst open. Eclairs splattered on the floor like pickup sticks.

Stevi gasped, "Are you okay?" She turned to Rosie. "I'm sorry I'm late." She scooped up the broken baked goods.

Rosie peered around the counter. "What's going on?"

The customer snapped, "This . . . this person ran me down."

Stevi scrabbled for her glasses. "I said I was sorry," she said, shoving them on.

Rosie's voice was cold. "I'll speak to you later, Stevi. I'm sorry for the inconvenience, Mrs. Johnston. Let me get you a new box of eclairs. I'll double your order for your trouble."

A new box of eclairs under her arm, Mrs. Johnston marched to the door. The bell tinkled. Mrs. Johnston stopped halfway through, turned back, and said, "I accept your apology, young lady."

"Thank you," said Stevi.

Rosie's angry face looked like a big red cherry. "I told you, I don't like tardiness. Don't let it happen again."

Stevi stared at the floor.

"Watch the counter while I take my break. I'll be in my office." Rosie stomped out.

Man, thought Stevi. *You'd think I killed somebody, the way Rosie is acting. I was only late.* She tied an apron around her waist, then stuffed her hair back into her hairnet. The bell tinkled, announcing another customer. Stevi stayed busy the rest of the evening.

The next few weeks settled into a routine. During the days she went to school, then did her homework when she got home. She worked two nights a week, Saturdays and one Sunday. Mona was always busy, so Stevi walked around the mall on her breaks by herself.

After school one Friday, Stevi and Mona were having a snack. Stevi stared at the blue flowers on the kitchen wallpaper. She asked, "Why don't you meet me at the mall to walk? After all, walking was your idea."

"I'm sorry, Stevi. I mean to walk with you. I just get involved and forget." Mona tilted her head. "Besides, if you're on a diet, why are you eating cookies?"

Stevi scowled, then shoved the cookies across the counter. "I don't know. I'm bored, I guess."

Mona finished her milk. "I belong to a fitness club. Would you like to go as my guest?"

"I've always been curious about them, but I couldn't afford to join one."

"If I take you as a guest, one of the instructors will work up a program for you," said Mona. "They'll try to sell you a membership but you can say no. We'll take your program card home and you can use it later."

"Isn't that stealing?" The idea *was* tempting.

"If you listen to the sales pitch, it isn't." Mona's eyes twinkled, as if devils were dancing in them. "Besides, Mom would be happy if I used my membership. I only go to meet the hunks around the swimming pool. I hate exercising."

Stevi laughed. *Who would it hurt?* "You've convinced me."

"You'll need exercise clothes, a bathing suit, and a towel. I keep my stuff in the trunk of my new car," said Mona.

"It's about time you took me for a ride," said Stevi. "You're lucky your parents can give you a car for your birthday." Stevi scribbled a note to her mom. "I just need a minute to get my sweats." She ran upstairs to her room.

Mona pulled her red Ford Miata into the club parking lot. She pointed to a good-looking guy entering the club. "Look, Stevi. Isn't he awesome? I told you this was fun."

"You're sick, Mona." Stevi smirked. "Don't you ever think of anything but guys?"

Mona's eyes were big and innocent. "Who me? Of course not!" She laughed. "Come on, girl friend, let's check out the action." She stumbled from the car, giggling.

Stevi struggled to pull her bulk from the sports car. The slim figures of the girls and women she saw entering the building gave her an attack of self-consciousness. She hesitated. Maybe this wasn't such a good idea after all. But Mona had already disappeared inside.

Red! The spa interior vibrated with it. The carpet was maroon; a chandelier hanging over a circular staircase had red light bulbs casting a rosy glow over the room. Walls and ceilings were painted white with red woodwork and doors.

Humid air smelled of chlorine and sweat. A glass wall on the left, fogged by an indoor pool in the next room, flickered with shadow people. In front of the foggy glass, was a health food bar. A muscular young man, in tight black pants and a white shirt trimmed in red, served a tall fruit drink to a leggy blonde in a Spandex body suit.

A tall thin woman, wearing a black and red body-hugging jump suit, greeted Mona and Stevi. "Good afternoon, may I see your membership cards, please?"

Mona whipped her card from her gym bag. "Stevi is my guest."

"Hi, Stevi. I'm Suzanne," said the blond-haired instructor. "Mona will show you the ladies' locker room. When you've changed, I'll show you the ladies' gym."

She and Mona strolled across the lobby to the first red door. Sweat, soap, makeup and hair spray smells swamped them in the pink dressing rooms. Mona pointed out the rest room and showers on the right.

She indicated a short door-lined hallway. "The glass door on the left is the sauna; the fogged one at the end is the steam room. On the right are the massage room and the sunlamps. Be sure you read the rules for using each facility. They can be dangerous."

Overwhelmed, Stevi said, "This must cost a lot."

"Not as much as you think," said Mona. "The members share the cost. If you're wealthy, you can afford your own gym at home. You change over there."

After changing into sweats, Stevi climbed the stairs to the ladies' gym. Suzanne then showed Stevi the indoor track, the men's gym, and the indoor and outdoor pools.

"Let's set up your workout," said Suzanne, leading Stevi to the gym office. "Before you start any new exercise program, you should get a checkup from your doctor. Let's get your measurements, then we'll get you started."

Reluctantly Stevi followed. Eyeing the skinny girls in leotards, she thought, *I feel like a watermelon in a cucumber patch.*

Chapter Nine

Suzanne's comment about getting a checkup before starting an exercise program weighed heavily on Stevi's mind. Dad was still out of work, so she couldn't bother her parents. *Maybe I should talk to the school nurse.*

She went to see Mrs. James during her next study hall. The school nurse was short and round, though not fat. Wavy brown hair with streaks of gray formed a halo around her face. Her brown eyes filled with sympathy and compassion as Stevi talked about her wish to lose weight. "Why do you overeat, Stevi?"

Puzzled, Stevi asked, "What do you mean? I eat because I'm hungry."

"Stop and think," said Mrs. James. "Are you hungry when you reach for food? Or are you bored, upset, angry or even tired?"

Stevi thought, *Have I ever been hungry?* She shook her head. "I never thought about it before."

Mrs. James smiled. "I'm not thin by any standard, but I'm not fat either. I used to be. I read a book called *Overcoming Overeating*. It changed my life.

"First, you must learn to accept yourself as you are. *Then,* you stop weighing yourself. *Overcoming Overeating* isn't a diet book. It teaches you to stop and examine why you eat. If you're hungry, fine. Eat anything you want. *But,* if you're upset, bored or angry, *stop and determine the reason.* Try to work through your problem, rather than eating. If you can't, and you still eat, *don't beat yourself up.* In time, you'll learn to eat only when your stomach is hungry."

Mrs. James wrote something on a slip of paper. "I want you to go to the library and get this book." She handed the paper to Stevi.

"I've read a bunch of diet books, Mrs. James. They haven't helped. My friend suggested exercise."

"Exercise *is* helpful," said Mrs. James. "But learning the reasons you overeat is essential if you want to control your weight for life."

"The whole concept sounds too good to be true," said Stevi. She clipped the paper into her notebook.

Mrs. James smiled. "It isn't easy. You have to make a commitment to a new way of life."

Stevi clutched her books to her chest, then started to get up.

"Sit back down for a minute, Stevi."

Oh no. Here comes the lecture. Anxious to leave, Stevi swung her feet making a scraping sound each time they touched the floor.

"Stevi, why do you wear baggy clothing? Is it to hide your weight?"

Stevi hung her head, hugging her books. She peeped at Mrs. James over the top of her glasses. "They're comfortable."

"Yes," said Mrs. James, smiling. "But they make you look bigger than you are. There are many clothes designed for heavier girls, now. You have a lovely face and beautiful hair. Your eyes are your best feature. You should consider wearing contact lenses and flattering clothes. You *could be* extremely attractive."

Stevi gently placed the books on her lap. She studied them to hide her tears. Softly, she said, "My dad's out of work. Money is tight at our house." She glanced into Mrs. James's kind eyes. "I have a job, but I give most of my paycheck to my family." She stood up. "I'll think over what you've said, though. Thanks for talking to me, Mrs. James."

The nurse smiled. "I'm sorry if I embarrassed you. I'm here if you need me." She slipped her arm around Stevi, while walking her to the door. "Good luck."

That evening, Mona and Stevi were discussing Stevi's visit to the school nurse. "Please come over and help me exercise," said Stevi.

"I know I said I'd be your coach," said Mona, "but my grandparents are having a fiftieth wedding anniversary party, and I have to go."

"You have more excuses than a computer has bytes," said Stevi. "Will you go shopping with me tomorrow? Mrs. James thinks I'd look better if I had some new clothes. I don't have any style sense; I need your help."

"I love shopping! I know *just* the store. I'll pick you up after school."

"You always pick me up since you've got the car." Stevi laughed. "Go to your party. If you hear funny huffing and puffing noises, it'll be me exercising. Later!"

Stevi sighed, then slowly climbed the stairs to her room. She was alone in the house. Silence hummed around her like the sound inside a seashell. *At least Nick isn't here to hassle me,* she thought as she changed into her sweats.

She stuck her feet under the edge of her bed, then started doing sit-ups. The first few were easy, but by the count of ten, she gasped for breath, then collapsed. In the silence, she heard a squeak, then a rustling like leaves. She listened. Nothing. *It must have been the wind.*

Turning around on the floor, she grasped one leg of the bed. Leg raises were easier than sit-ups. Panting, she counted to fifteen. Wet and sweaty, she dragged herself from the floor to sprawl on her bed, where she studied the program card from the spa.

Next on her exercise list was a combination stretch. She was to put her leg on a bar and bend over from the waist like a dancer. Her room didn't have a bar. Glancing around, she searched for a substitute, then decided to use her desk chair. The back was a bit high, but she thought she could manage.

She pulled the chair into the middle of the room, then piled books on the seat to keep it steady. Hoisting her leg up, she hooked her ankle over the back of the chair, and stretched toward her toes. She could barely touch her knees. Disgusted, she mumbled, "You can do it. Try harder."

She heard a bump, then the sound of muffled laughter outside her door. *Someone must have come home. I'd better close my bedroom door.*

She tried to lift her leg. It wouldn't move. "Darn!" With both hands, she grabbed her leg trying to lift it. Nothing happened. She tried to slide her leg off the back of the chair.

Giggles erupted from the hall landing.

"Who's there?" The leg Stevi was standing on ached.

Whispers, then more giggles.

"Help, I'm stuck." She tried twisting to see who was watching. Her arms swung like windmills to keep her balance. She froze, trying to hear what was happening in the hall.

This time she could hear. "I told you watching the fatty was worth twenty-five cents."

There are several people out there. Stevi tried again to move. *This is ridiculous.*

"Nick, you dweeb. Help me." Tears of humiliation filled Stevi's eyes. "Please help me," she pleaded.

Nick snickered, then gasped, "J-just t-turn the c-chair over."

How dumb can I be? She tilted the chair toward her. Her leg came unhooked. The books crashed to the floor with Stevi sprawled on top of them.

"We'd better get out of here before she gets up," said Nick.

Stevi rolled over in time to see Nick and several friends disappear down the stairway. Sobbing, Stevi slammed her bedroom door shut. "I'll never exercise again!"

Chapter Ten

After school the next day, Stevi and Mona drove to the Lovely Lady Boutique. "This is a special shop," said Mona, opening the door. "They specialize in the latest fashions, but they only buy one outfit in each size. If they don't have your size they order it for you."

"Sounds expensive," muttered Stevi.

Mona shrugged. "It is, but you often find look-alikes at less expensive stores. Lovely Lady carries the type of clothing you see on TV."

Stevi glanced at the price tag on a blouse. She gasped. "There's no way I can afford to shop here! It would take me a month to earn this much."

"Forget the price tags. Just try on the clothes and find out what style looks good on you." Mona rifled through a clothing rack. She pulled out a blue silk pantsuit and a print blouse. "Try these on."

Stevi shook her head. "I can't wear this size."

Mona smiled. "Sure you can. Expensive clothing sizes run larger than inexpensive sizes."

Stevi raised an eyebrow in disbelief, shrugged, then took the suit to the dressing room. *I'd never have believed it.* She stared at herself in a full-length mirror. She heard Mona telling the saleslady they were just looking. Her attention riveted to the mirror; she turned right, then left. *I look ten pounds thinner. I never knew clothing could make so much difference.*

"Come out and let me see," said Mona. Stevi timidly stepped from the dressing room. "You look awesome!" Mona handed her a maroon skirt and soft pink sweater. "Try these."

Gently gathered at the waist, the wool skirt gave the impression of fullness, but without extra material that adds width to a heavy person's appearance. The lacy, blushing-pink sweater brought out the color in Stevi's cheeks, and provided a striking contrast with her dark wavy hair. Tiny pink pearls were woven into a softly draped neckline. It was the most beautiful sweater Stevi had ever seen. Dreamily, Stevi closed her eyes and imagined Ari's reaction if he saw her in it.

Mona stuck her head into the dressing room. "That would be perfect for the Christmas dance at school this year."

"Right," said Stevi, sadly. "Who is going to ask *me*?" *I finally find something I look good in, and now I can't afford it. If I could only lose weight so I could look good in regular clothes like everyone else. . . .*

Mona said, "I'm going to try on a couple of things."

"Okay," said Stevi. Back in her own drab clothing, she gazed at her ugly reflection. Dead inside, she hung the maroon skirt and pink sweater back on the rack.

Mona purchased a blouse. She and Stevi were halfway across the parking lot when Mona said, "I forgot something." She handed Stevi her car keys. "Unlock the car. I'll be right back."

Stevi sauntered to the car, opened it and crawled in. Staring into space she daydreamed. *If only I could go to sleep some night and wake up thin the next morning. I wish there were an easy way to lose weight.*

Mona raced to the car, threw her Lovely Lady bag into the backseat and jumped inside. Face flushed, her hands shook so badly she couldn't get her key into the car's ignition at first. "Let's get out of here."

Mona jammed the car into gear, then pulled into traffic so quickly she almost hit another car. The driver yelled, then made an obscene gesture. "Oh, chill out," Mona screamed back.

Clutching the seat, fear sliced through Stevi. "What's the hurry, Mona? You almost caused an accident!"

The car raced down the highway. Mona began to giggle until she could barely breathe. Her pupils were huge, making her blue eyes appear black. Stevi thought Mona was going to choke when she spit out, "The maroon outfit . . ."

"What about it?"

Mona indicated the shopping bag in the back seat. "I've got a surprise for you." She pitched the bag to Stevi.

Fear engulfed Stevi, making her cold. Her heart raced. *What had Mona done?* Hands trembling, she opened the bag. Wadded inside were the maroon skirt and pink sweater.

"Mona?"

Mona's face glowed. In her excitement, her foot plunged down on the accelerator. "What a high," she sang. "I've never ripped *that* shop off before."

Stevi gasped, wiped clammy hands on her jeans, then thought, *The police . . . jail . . . my parents will kill me if we get caught.* She whispered, "What am I going to tell my parents?"

"Why tell your parents anything? Cut the tags off and hang the outfit in the back of your closet. You can say you've had it forever."

Stevi's mind reeled. Staring out the car window, she suddenly realized how fast they were going. At that moment, the traffic light turned red. She screamed. "Slow down, Mona!"

The car screeched through the intersection before Mona braked. "Sorry." Mona laughed. "That was fun."

Stevi's heart slowed. *I can't take the outfit back. If I do, they'd think I stole it. If I take it home, I'll be an accomplice.* She didn't know what to do. She didn't have the money to pay for it. Her stomach rumbled; she wished she had something to eat.

Mona glanced at Stevi. "Hey, girl friend, don't look so miserable. I only took the clothes to make you happy. Shoplifting's no big deal."

Stevi shook her head, frustrated that Mona didn't understand. "I need to lose weight, not get a police record."

"My mom takes diet pills," said Mona. "Want me to get you some? Mom swears by them."

"Aren't they dangerous? Habit forming?"

"Heck no! Mom's doctor wouldn't give them to her if they were. Try 'em. If you don't like them, you don't have to take any more."

When Stevi didn't reply, Mona continued. "There's another option."

"What's that?"

"Crack's good for losing weight. I know someone who uses it all the time. She's skinny as a rail. Says she's never hungry."

"You must be kidding. *Crack's dangerous!* I'd never use it. Besides, isn't it expensive? Anyway . . . I wouldn't know where to get it."

"A girl in school sells. Even you can afford crack," said Mona.

"FORGET CRACK! I'd rather take diet pills." She sighed unhappily. "Pills *would* be easier than exercising."

Chapter Eleven

Later that evening, Mona telephoned Stevi. "Some of us are going horseback riding Saturday. Do you want to come?"

"I have to work."

"Call in sick. Everybody does it."

Stevi hesitated. "Okay. I *have* been working hard. I deserve a break."

"When you go to work Thursday night, pretend you don't feel well." Stevi heard mischief in Mona's voice. "Then when you call in Saturday, no one will suspect anything."

Saturday dawned cool and crisp, not a cloud in the sky. Brilliant sunlight brought everything into sharp focus in the clear autumn air. Walking toward the bus stop, Stevi thought it was a perfect day for horseback riding.

Mona parked her car next to the bus stop. Loud music blared from the car radio. She tapped her fingers on the steering wheel to the beat of the music. Every few seconds she glanced at her watch.

Stevi opened the curbside door. "What a wonderful day to ditch work!" Leaning against the car, she peeled oversized work slacks from the faded jeans underneath. "I didn't want my parents to suspect I wasn't working."

Mona eased the car into the light Saturday traffic. The breeze blowing through the open window ruffled her long blond hair. "We're picking up Carin and Terrina. Jake is picking up the guys."

"Have you ever been riding at this place before?"

"No, but Jesse knows the owner. I haven't ridden much. I hope I get a gentle horse," said Mona.

Mona stopped the car in front of Carin's house, a large ranch style set back from the road. Brightly colored mums filled neat gardens. Giggling, Carin and Terrina strolled down the blacktop driveway in matching "We're Available" sweat shirts and jeans.

Riding down the highway, the girls chatted about boys, how pretty the fall leaves were, and wondered if they'd missed the sign to the stables.

"No," Carin squealed. "There's the sign."

Mona turned the car into a long pothole-filled driveway. An ancient farmhouse sat at the top of a steep hill. The car bounced up the road, past the house, then crawled to a stop on a gravel parking area. Tied to a fence badly in need of paint, several tired-looking horses stood under the biggest oak tree Stevi had ever seen. Behind the tree was a run-down barn, once red but now faded gray. Its walls had large gaps where siding had rotted away. The entire farm reeked of age and neglect.

Stevi nervously searched for Ari. "I guess we're the first ones here."

The girls tumbled from the car. A bowlegged man in dusty, torn jeans led another horse from the barn. He tied the horse with the others, then ambled toward the girls. He wore a faded, rumpled red and green plaid shirt and a shapeless old cowboy hat stuck on the back of his stringy brown hair. He needed a shave and a haircut. "Howdy, ladies. What can I do fer ya?"

The smell of hay and manure drifted to Stevi's nose. "We're Jesse's friends," said Mona. "He and some other friends are going to meet us to go riding."

"Yer early," said the cowboy. "Name's Jim." He nodded toward the huddled girls. "I hav'ta finish saddlin' the ponies. Make yerselves comfortable until the rest of the gang gets here." He ambled back toward the barn.

All the girls exchanged glances. They smiled, then giggled.

"Like out of a movie," sputtered Mona.

A cloud of dust billowed up the dirt driveway. Jake's Chevy skidded to a stop, spraying gravel. Jake, Ari, Brian and Jesse sprang from the car. Stevi's eyes were drawn to Ari's jeaned and cowboy-shirted body. Goose bumps ran up her arms. *He's so handsome.* Ari noticed Stevi staring and winked.

Jim led another horse from the barn.

"Hey, Jim!" Jesse sprinted toward his friend. They shook hands.

"Any of yer friends experienced riders?" Jim studied the young people. "Besides you, Jesse?"

Stevi stepped forward. "I've been riding most of my life."

Jim acknowledged her, then pulled some crumpled papers from his back pocket. "Y'all got to sign these papers, sayin' yer ridin' at yer own risk. Jesse, yer in charge, since I know ya."

Jesse saluted. "You got it, Jim."

The teens mounted. Jesse proudly said, "Follow me, dudes." He rode ahead. Jake and Mona followed, riding together.

Carin's horse balked. Stevi said, "Give it a kick."

"Thanks," said Carin. Carin's horse started, then Brian's and Terrina's horses followed with Stevi and Ari bringing up the rear. The horses formed a ragged line as they clopped down the hill, behind the old barn.

Swaying in the saddle, Stevi surveyed the landscape. A wide brook snaked through a gully at the bottom of the hill. Across a pasture, the trail led up another hill then disappeared into woods.

Jesse rode across the stream without incident. Carin followed, but Jake's horse stopped for a drink. Terrina, Brian and Ari passed Jake. Stevi said, "It's not good for him to drink too much while we're riding." She urged her horse into a trot to catch the others.

"Jesse, how do I make this animal go?" Jake laughed. "I can't find the accelerator."

Jesse swung his horse around, removing his belt as he galloped toward Jake.

Stevi turned in her saddle and spotted Jesse's raised arm. "NO," she screamed, as the belt came down.

TH-WACK.

Jake's horse squealed, then plunged from the stream in a fast trot. Jake grabbed the pommel, bouncing up and down like popcorn in a hot skillet. His feet slipped free of the stirrups, flopping and kicking the horse into a full gallop. He screamed, "W-w-where's t-t-the b-b-brake?"

Ari's horse, spooked by the noise, also broke into a run. Ari's face turned greenish from fear. "HELP!"

Jesse, who was galloping the wrong direction, wheeled his horse and gave chase.

Everyone froze, except Stevi. A quick glance at Jesse told her he'd never catch both runaway horses. She kicked her mount viciously and thundered past her friends.

Stevi hugged her horse's neck, like a jockey, urging him faster. The wind and the horse's billowing mane took her breath away. She'd almost caught Ari, when Jake's horse lifted his tail and defecated.

Ari, looking over his shoulder at Stevi, didn't see what was coming. Stevi yelled, "Ari, duck."

Off balance, Ari turned just in time to get a large smelly splatter across the front of his shirt.

Stevi grabbed Ari's reins, pulling their horses to a stop. Jake was riding toward a tree with low-hanging branches. "Watch out, Jake!"

THUNK. The tree limb hit Jake squarely across the side of his head. Swept from his horse, for one frozen moment he hung in the air. Then he dropped.

Stevi scrambled from her saddle. She ran to Jake's crumpled body lying in the leaves. He didn't move.

Jesse raced up, followed by Brian and the girls. "Is he all right?"

Jake stared up, not moving.

"Can you move?"

"Is anything broken?

Stevi asked, "Should I go for an ambulance?"

Slowly, Jake moved his arms, then his legs. His face was pale. Surprise flickered into his eyes. "I only bruised my pride," he said, sitting up. He looked at Jesse. "You didn't warn me the trees could reach out and touch me."

Chapter Twelve

Jake dusted himself off. "I want to rest under a shady tree for a while."

"Sounds good to me," said Mona. "I'm still shaking."

Ari tugged at his shirt. "I need to rinse this in the stream. Come with me, Stevi?" She nodded eagerly, heart pounding. "Thanks for rescuing me."

"Any experienced rider could have done it."

Ari struggled out of his shirt. "You must ride a lot."

Stevi stared at Ari's golden-colored chest. "I've been riding all my life," said Stevi. "I started before I could walk. I was born on a farm. Where were you born?"

Squatting at the edge of the stream, Ari rinsed the brown stain from his shirt. "In Vietnam," he said, softly.

Stunned, Stevi didn't know what to say. Ari stood up, slipping on the damp shirt, but left it unbuttoned to dry. "Let's see if the others are ready to ride yet."

They trudged up the hill. Stevi heard Brian ask, "Jake, are you all right?"

Mona had her arms around Jake who was shaking violently.

Terrina leaned forward. "What's wrong with him? Should we go for a doctor?"

"He may be in shock," Stevi guessed. "Keep him warm."

Carin produced a vial of crack. "I've got something to take the edge off."

Jake stared at the vial. "Yeah . . . sounds good to me."

"I don't know," said Jesse. He looked troubled. "I've never done crack before."

Carin laughed. "Nothing to it."

"I'm curious," said Brian. "I've always wondered what the fuss was about."

Stevi searched the faces of her friends. She didn't want to be different, but had to speak up. "Jake shouldn't take drugs after a fall." No one listened to her.

Ari slipped his arm around Stevi's waist. "Let's go riding. Isn't that what we came for?"

Thankfully, Stevi nodded.

"I'm staying here," said Mona. "I don't care if I never get on another horse." She glanced questioningly at Terrina.

Terrina shrugged. "I'll stay." Jesse nodded, too.

Shaking his head, Ari led Stevi to the horses. "Leave them to their fun."

Frowning, Stevi glanced over her shoulder. "I can't believe they're doing crack. Don't they realize how dangerous it is?"

"They've heard all the warnings." They mounted. "You lead the way," Ari said. "Just go slowly, please. I'm not sure I have the hang of this riding stuff."

They rode in silence until the path forked. One branch descended a steep rocky hill, the other curved into a thickly wooded area. Stevi stopped. "Which way?"

Ari studied both routes. "The woods. I'm not ready for a steep trail."

When the track widened, Ari urged his mount forward. "I wanted to say thanks again. I think you're brave."

Cheeks burning, Stevi said, "Horses can tell inexperienced riders. They'll try to get away with anything they can."

Stevi didn't know how to keep the conversation going. They

fell silent until they came to a rusted iron fence surrounding a cemetery.

Ari asked, "Want to investigate?"

They dismounted, tied their horses, then pushed open the gate which hung from one hinge. Stevi shivered. "This place gives me the creeps."

Headstones lay cocked at different angles, like unruly hair, with tall weeds and grass growing around them. Vines hung from tree branches that trailed over the fence. "All this place needs is fog and Spanish moss to be the setting for a horror movie," said Stevi. She giggled nervously, then stepped closer to Ari.

Ari brushed dirt and weeds from a headstone so he could read the inscription. "Awesome!" He scrambled from grave to grave. "This place is ancient. The most recent date is 1903."

Chills ran up and down Stevi's spine. "I'm scared. Can we leave?"

Ari stood and smiled. "I think it's neat."

"Why?"

His black eyes glittered in the sunlight. "When you're adopted like I am, any kind of family history is interesting."

Surprised, Stevi said, "I didn't know you were adopted."

Ari shrugged. "My mom died in Vietnam when I was a baby. I came here, and my parents adopted me."

"Wow. Do you know your birth father?"

"I know he's an American. That's why I was sent here. Dad left a kid in Nam, too. Since he couldn't find his real kid, he adopted me."

"I don't know what to say, Ari, except I'm glad you're here."

Ari looked fierce. "Don't feel sorry for me. I'm one of the lucky ones."

Ari's defensive attitude was bewildering. "We'd better ride back to the others," Stevi said, returning to the horses.

When they got back, they dismounted, leaving their horses to graze in the meadow with the rest of the horses. They strolled over to their friends. Jake had apparently recovered and was necking with Mona. Giggles came from a nearby clump of bushes. Stevi guessed Terrina and Jesse were making out, too.

Brian leaned against a tree with Carin's head in his lap. Stevi sat in the grass near them. Carin smiled seductively at Ari. "Have a good ride?" Carin's words were slurred.

She sounds either drunk or high. Stevi remembered times in school when Carin had acted strangely.

Ari stood with a foolish grin on his face.

Carin staggered to her feet, and threw herself into Ari's arms. She gazed into his eyes. "Want to take a walk?"

Brian winked at Ari. "Go ahead. I'll keep Stevi company."

Giggling, Carin wobbled and almost fell. Ari's arms tightened around her. He glanced over his shoulder. "Later, dudes."

Stevi wanted to throw something at Carin. Instead, she jumped to her feet and snarled, "I'm going to check on the horses." She stomped off. *I HAVE to lose weight if I want to keep Ari's interest.* Suddenly, Mona's diet pills sounded really interesting.

Chapter Thirteen

 Several weeks later, Stevi worked the Sunday shift at the bakery by herself. After four hours, she was still full of energy and hadn't gotten hungry. *These diet pills really work,* she thought, while bagging an order.

Her customer was discussing a party she had planned for that evening when two old women entered the bakery. They began inspecting the baked goods as if they were from the health department.

One woman, dressed in a battleship-gray suit and matching feathered hat, pointed to the fruit-filled pastries. "Hilda," she said loudly, "what flavor are those yellow ones?"

Hilda, dressed in deep red, shrugged. "I don't know."

"Miss," shouted the gray lady, "what flavor are these pastries?"

Irritated, Stevi growled, "They're lemon. I'll be with you in a moment." She concentrated on what her customer was saying.

"Give me two dozen chocolate chip cookies," said the party lady.

Hilda pointed to the filled donuts. "What's inside these, Milly?"

Milly yelled, "Girl, Hilda wants to know what's inside the donuts?"

Stevi's hands shook; she counted to ten. "I'll help you in a minute," she said through gritted teeth. "How many cookies did you want?"

Milly looked into the coffee-cake counter. *"I want to know how much these cakes are,"* she insisted.

"I *said* I'd be with you in a moment," snapped Stevi. She apologized to her customer, then finished waiting on her.

As the party lady left, Hilda said to Milly, "Aren't some people impertinent?"

"All young people are that way. In our day, young people had good manners," Milly replied.

Pivoting, Stevi snarled, "You're old enough to know better than to interrupt. Where'd you learn *your* manners, in a gutter?"

The old ladies blanched. Stevi knew she'd gone too far.

"Come on, Hilda," said Milly stiffly. "Let's get out of here."

Hilda pointed a bony finger at Stevi. "You haven't heard the last of this, young woman." Backs straight, noses in the air, the old women stomped out.

"Good riddance," Stevi hissed. The bell announced another customer and Stevi put the incident from her mind.

Tuesday night when she came to work, Stevi was in a cheerful mood. The little bell tinkled merrily as she bounced in, waving to Rosie.

Rosie asked another salesgirl to finish waiting on her customer. "Stevi," she said, "I want to speak to you in my office, *right now!"*

What'd I do? Stevi scratched her head as she followed Rosie's waddling figure.

"Why did you insult Hilda Hoffman, Sunday?"

"I don't know what you're talking about," said Stevi.

"Hilda Hoffman, the store owner's mother. She said you were rude and wouldn't wait on her and her friend," said Rosie. "What do you have to say for yourself?"

Stevi frowned, then remembered. "Oh, the two cranky old ladies." She explained what had happened.

"That's *no excuse*. The customer is *always* right. I've had other complaints about your short temper, dearie. Change your attitude or you will be looking for another job." Rosie waddled out of the office.

"It's always my fault," fumed Stevi. "If I didn't need the money, I'd quit!"

"Get in here, Stevi. I'm paying you to work," called Rosie. Still seething, Stevi started her shift.

On her break Stevi marched around the mall trying to let off steam. Her mind still on the reprimand, she blindly bumped into someone. "Watch it buddy!"

"Hey dude, what's the hurry?" It was Ari! Eyes twinkling, he said, "Are you having a bad day?"

Ari's smile made Stevi boil. *How dare he act like nothing happened!* He hadn't spoken to her since they went horseback riding. He'd been too busy with Carin.

"It might help to talk about it," said Ari.

"You've helped enough already!" Stevi's eyes flashed, her hands were clenched. She wanted to punch him.

Ari's smile faded. He stepped back. "What did I say?"

"Forget it." Stevi stomped away.

Ari grabbed her arm. "What's wrong? Let me help."

He looked so eager, for a moment Stevi almost forgave him. Then she remembered Carin. "Leave me alone."

"Women! I don't need the hassle." Ari turned away.

"Neither do I," Stevi said, stomping her foot. Watching his retreating back, a sense of loss overwhelmed her. *What's wrong with me? Why am I so angry?* She ran after him. "Ari, I'm sorry. Let me explain."

He stopped, face rigid. "So explain."

"I just got chewed out at work," said Stevi, pacing back and forth. "I'm sorry, I shouldn't take it out on my friends. Forgive me?"

Ari shrugged. "I guess so." He glanced at his watch. "I have to get going. See you around." He stalked away.

Stevi blinked back tears. *He's still angry, and I don't blame him. Why do I get so angry and upset lately?* She trudged back to the bakery, but her mind was on Ari the rest of the evening.

After work Stevi found a message to call Mona taped on

her bedroom door. She rushed to the telephone in the upstairs hall.

"Did he ask you?" demanded Mona.

"What are you talking about?"

"Did Ari ask you to the Christmas dance? He said he was coming to the mall to ask you," said Mona.

"I ran into Ari, but he didn't ask me to the dance." Stevi explained what had happened.

"You dweeb! You finally lose some weight, and Ari finally notices and asks you out, then you blow it. What's the matter with you?"

Stevi started to cry. "I don't know, Mona. I lose my temper when I don't mean to, or I burst into tears for no reason. I feel like a spring that's wound too tight." She ran her hand through her hair. "Am I losing my mind?"

"It's the diet pills," said Mona. "Mom gets like that, too. But look—you're thinner. Have you noticed how much better you look lately?"

Stevi sagged against the wall. "Is it worth it, if I lose all my friends?"

Chapter Fourteen

Saturday, Stevi rummaged through her closet searching for something that fit to wear to work. Jogging shoes, tattered jeans, old ice skates, faded stuffed animals, books and papers flew over her shoulder. She found the maroon skirt and pink sweater Mona had stolen for her. Guilt rippled to the surface of her mind.

She held the skirt to her waist. It seemed big. She slipped it over her head; the waistband drooped low on her hips. *It's too big! When did this happen? I've never even worn it.*

Full of relief, she smiled. *Now that I'm smaller, I don't have to wear it.* She jammed the skirt across a coat hanger and shoved it back into her closet. Finally, she found a pair of old slacks she hadn't worn in years. They fit.

She finished dressing, her thoughts on the bakery. She hated working there; it was so hard to ignore the cookies and donuts. She wished she could find a job where she wasn't around food all the time.

Rosie was glassy-eyed with fatigue in the crowded bakery that evening. "Hurry up, Stevi. We need help," she said.

Scowling, Stevi replied, "I'm early. I don't start for another fifteen minutes."

"I want you to start now," demanded Rosie.

Sullenly, Stevi strolled into the back room. She freshened her makeup, took a diet pill, and went to the rest room. When she finished it was her normal starting time. Full of false energy, she flew from customer to customer, her voice sharp and unfriendly as she rushed them from the bakery. When the last customer left, Stevi sagged against the counter. "This is the busiest I've ever seen the place," she said to Rosie.

Rosie's face was red. She breathed hard as if she'd been running. Her eyes snapped with anger. She spoke deliberately, as if to a naughty child. "If I say I want you to start early, I mean *right now,* not fifteen minutes from now."

Startled, Stevi straightened. "We got everyone taken care of. What's your beef?"

"You were rude and abrupt to the customers." Rosie wagged a pudgy finger at Stevi. "I don't like your attitude lately."

"I don't know what you're talking about." Stevi stood feet apart, hands on hips. "I haven't changed. You're picking on me because you're tired. That's not fair. I do a good job for you."

"Don't talk back to *me,* young lady," Rosie sputtered. "I'm warning you for the last time. If you don't change your attitude, you're fired."

"You don't have to warn me anymore," Stevi shouted. She snatched her hairnet off and threw it at Rosie. "I quit!" Grabbing her purse from the back room, she raced from the bakery. The sound of the tinkling bell on the door brought tears to her eyes.

"Why?" she berated herself as she paced the mall. Already she regretted her burst of temper. "I've got to stop taking those dumb pills. I was never like this before." She wondered if Rosie would forgive her. She stalked up and down the mall the rest of the evening, cooling off and trying to decide what to do. At her normal quitting time, she boarded the bus for home.

As she climbed the front steps, laughter floated on the night air. Her whole family was gathered in the living room laughing and hugging each other. Stevi stopped in the doorway. "What's going on?"

"Your dad got his job back," Mom said. She hugged Stevi.

"I'm happy for you," Stevi said, her voice flat. No one noticed her lack of enthusiasm. Feeling isolated, she slowly climbed the stairs to her room. "I'm a failure," she mumbled. "Now I understand how Dad must have felt. Maybe I won't tell them I quit for a few days."

Lying in the dark, she listened to her mother's happy laughter drifting up the stairwell. "It'll take a few weeks to get the bills caught up," said Mom, "but with Stevi's help it'll go faster."

Stevi closed her door softly. *They're depending on me.* She replayed the scene with Rosie in her head. *It's the pills. If only I'd kept my temper. No more pills for me.*

The next morning at school, Stevi was so tired—picking up a pencil was a chore. She hadn't had any appetite at breakfast, but by lunchtime she was starving. After eating the lunch Mom had packed, she bought two slices of pecan pie from the school cafeteria. Stevi devoured one and was starting the second when Mona pulled up a chair.

Mona broke off a chunk of pie crust then shoved it into her mouth. "Why are you eating pie?"

"I'm hungry," Stevi snapped.

"Did you forget your pill this morning? I have a couple in my purse, if you need one."

Stevi stopped chewing. "I quit my job yesterday, and I'm not taking any more pills."

Mona's hand stopped halfway to her mouth. Her eyes widened. "What happened?"

Stevi told her. "The pills make me jittery, and I hate the person I'm becoming."

"But Stevi, you look awesome. Your pants are baggy and your face isn't round anymore. Why give up a good thing?"

A lump formed in Stevi's throat. She swallowed. "It's not worth it. I never had many friends to start with, now I only have you. What's the use of being thin if I'm unhappy and no one likes me?"

Mona shook her head, disgust written on her face. "You're never satisfied, are you? Do you really know what you want?" Shoving her chair back she left. Stevi stared after her.

"Great, now I've alienated my only friend!" She glared at her watch. Fifteen minutes until the next class.

Troubled, she walked to the candy machine. Inserting her money she filled her pockets with candy bars. Her shoulders drooped as she peeled the wrapper from a chocolate bar. Standing in the middle of the hall, she closed her eyes and took a bite. Sweetness filled her mouth—then her mind. It felt like renewing an old friendship.

Chapter Fifteen

By Thursday evening, Stevi still hadn't told her parents she'd quit her job. She dressed for work, as usual, taking the bus to the mall. *What if someone who knows my parents notices I'm not working and tells them?* Stevi stopped at the Pizza Crib to buy a slice of pizza. As she ate, she strolled through the mall. Standing in front of the Awesome Rags Teen Shop, she licked the last bite of cheese from her fingers.

She wondered if she could wear junior sizes? She wanted to try, but she'd been bingeing the last few days. . . . She didn't have any money, either. "What the heck," she muttered, then entered the store.

She found two pairs of jeans and a soft knit shirt in her favorite shade of blue. The dressing room checker counted the garments. Inside, Stevi chose the last dressing stall, pulling its green curtain for privacy. Her reflection stared at her from a full-length mirror.

She frowned at her baggy slacks and oversized sweater before stripping them off. She slipped into the smaller-sized jeans. They wouldn't button, but the larger size fit her perfectly and looked wonderful with the blue shirt. "I've changed," Stevi mumbled, perusing her thinner self in the mirror. Suddenly, anger swelled inside like a hot-air balloon. "I can't afford these, but will anyone like me if I keep looking like a dweeb?"

She yanked her baggy pants and sweater over the store's jeans and shirt. Blood raced in her veins; her heart pounded. A quick glance in the mirror to make sure the new jeans and shirt were hidden . . . then she walked out—past the checker whose back was turned—and out of the store into the mall.

Scared but excited, Stevi raced down a maintenance hall to a rest room. Inside a stall, she peeled off her baggy clothes and rolled them into a ball. She stripped the tags from her new jeans and shirt, then stepped from the stall and threw her old clothing into the trash.

She caught sight of herself in the mirror. Her dark eyes were shining; her cheeks were pink as if she'd just come in from a brisk autumn day. The blue shirt brought out the highlights in her dark hair. She'd never looked so good.

I'll go back to Awesome Rags and ask for a job! For the first time since she'd lost her old one, she was alive. Head held high, Stevi marched into the store and asked the cashier for a job application.

The application was easy to fill out this time. A tingle of fear ran down her spine as she introduced herself to the manager, but Mrs. Laird didn't recognize her. Smiling, she answered Mrs. Laird's questions. The interview was a breeze; she got the job.

Stevi felt a twinge of guilt over the shoplifting, but she pushed it from her mind. She was high . . . excited, as if flying; colors were brighter. *This must be what it's like to be on drugs.* She grinned at everyone she met. *Now* she could tell Mom and Dad she'd quit the bakery.

The following Monday, Stevi wore her new jeans to work. Her old clothes were either too big or too small. She wondered if the theft had been discovered. Her hands were sweaty and cold as she entered the store.

"Good evening," said Mrs. Laird.

Stevi's voice quivered as she replied, "Evening."

Mrs. Laird ran her hand through her curly brown hair, pushing it back from her face. The store lights reflected off her glasses, hiding her eyes from Stevie. "The most important part of your job, next to waiting on customers, is watching for shoplifters," said Mrs. Laird.

Stevi's heart pounded. *She knows.*

"Our store loses hundreds of dollars in merchandise every week to shoplifting," Mrs. Laird continued.

Stevi wiped clammy hands on her jeans. She forced words from frozen lips, "H-how will I recognize a shoplifter?"

"Watch for people carrying large bags, or wearing baggy clothing or coats, who look nervous. We just caught a seventy-five-year-old grandmother who wanted a present for her granddaughter but didn't want to spend her money," said Mrs. Laird. "They come in all shapes, sizes and ages."

Knees weak, Stevi asked, "What should I do if I see a shoplifter?" The conversation was making her ill.

"Usually, if you walk over and ask to help, the shoplifter will change her mind. She'll leave if she knows you're watching. *If* she's already taken something, tell me so I can call security. *Never* try to stop shoplifters yourself."

Stevi nodded.

"Your first job is dressing room checker," said Mrs. Laird. "Count the number of garments going in, then coming out. Give the customer a matching number tag and never leave the dressing room unattended. Any questions?"

Stevi shook her head.

What a dilemma. My job is to stop shoplifting, but I'm wearing stolen clothes. How will I straighten this mess out?

Stevi worked every night for the next two weeks. Each time she entered the store, her guilt ate at her. Her stomach burned, and she had nightmares when she tried to sleep. She ate candy to calm her nerves. Every time she looked up and saw Mrs. Laird watching her, she was sure the woman knew her guilty secret.

On the bus ride home, after receiving her first paycheck, Stevi mulled over her problem. "I love working at Awesome Rags," said Stevi, talking to herself. "Mrs. Laird is a wonderful boss, but if I tell her what I did she'll fire me." Chilled, she hugged herself. "But I just can't live with this guilt."

"I have to make things right," she mumbled. The lady sitting next to her looked at her strangely.

Chapter Sixteen

Monday morning, Stevi called Awesome Rags from school. "Mrs. Laird, may I speak to you privately when I get to work tonight."

"Can you come in half an hour early, Stevi?"

"Yes ma'am."

"I'll see you in my office then. Have a good day, Stevi."

That evening, Stevi stopped outside Mrs. Laird's office. *I hope she can't see how badly I'm shaking.* Stevi squared her shoulders. *I can do this. I have to make things right.* She twisted the doorknob and stepped inside.

Mrs. Laird motioned toward the chair. "What did you want to talk about?"

Stevi's mouth was dry, her tongue like sandpaper. She licked her lips and tried to speak. Nothing came out.

Mrs. Laird smiled encouragement. "Stevi, do you like your job?"

Stevi nodded. "Oh yes ma'am." She stared at her lap, her fingers twisting her purse strap. "That's the problem; I don't want to lose it," she whispered, then peeped over her glasses.

Mrs. Laird looked puzzled.

"I did a really dumb thing." Stevi spoke fast. "It was the first and only time—I swear—and I'll never do it again. I want to make it right. Please understand and give me another chance."

"This sounds serious, Stevi," said Mrs. Laird, frowning. "You'd better start at the beginning."

Stevi stared at her feet. "I used to work at Butterball Bakery." Her voice quivered. "I got the job because I was fat. I started taking diet pills, but they made me irritable and I couldn't keep my temper. I was rude to customers.

"I had an argument with Rosie, my boss, and I quit in a fit of anger. Trying to make myself feel better, I came into Awesome Rags to see if I'd lost enough weight to wear junior clothes. The dressing room attendant turned her back. I walked out with a pair of jeans and a shirt, and I've felt guilty ever since." She glanced up. Mrs. Laird looked furious. "Please don't fire me. I don't take pills anymore and I love working here."

"I should call the police," Mrs. Laird said, "plus fire you."

Stevi hung her head. In a small voice she said, "I deserve whatever I get. I'll pay for the outfit I took from my paycheck." She looked into Mrs. Laird's eyes. "I'm sorry— I'll never steal again, and if you give me another chance, I'll be the best employee you've ever had. I promise." She waited.

After a while, the expression on Mrs. Laird's face softened. "Okay, I'll give you a chance—*but* you're on probation for six months. One mistake and you're gone."

Stevi let out the breath she didn't know she was holding. Light-headed, she grinned. "Thank you. You'll never be sorry." She clutched her purse, ready to leave, but Mrs. Laird asked her to stay.

"Weight dominates your life, doesn't it, Stevi? Would you discuss this with me?"

Stevi felt embarrassed, but realized Mrs. Laird cared. She nodded.

Mrs. Laird asked, "Have you read *Overcoming Overeating* or *It's Not What You Eat, It's What's Eating You*?"

"I've heard of the first one," said Stevi. Scowling, she tried to remember. "I think the school nurse mentioned it."

"The medical community is beginning to realize there's a lot more to weight control than dieting. Dieting itself can cause you to gain weight."

"I didn't know that," said Stevi.

Mrs. Laird tapped a pencil on the desk, then continued. "When you diet, you change your eating habits *temporarily.* Later, after you've lost weight, you go back to your old eating habits and end up weighing more than before. Each time you diet, it gets harder to lose."

Stevi leaned forward. "Then what can I do?"

Grinning, Mrs. Laird said, "You have to learn to tell the difference between physiological—or real—hunger and eating for comfort. Most overweight people use food to manage anxiety.

"*Overcoming Overeating* teaches you to put food back where it belongs. You learn how to lose weight by relearning to eat. Their three-part plan teaches you to free yourself from society's conception of how you should look and feel. Then, you learn how, why, when and what to eat. In the third phase, you learn to understand your emotional life and how it relates to eating.

"*It's Not What You Eat, It's What's Eating You* isn't a diet book, though it does suggest a simple old-fashioned calorie diet. It's a twenty-eight-day plan for understanding your underlying emotions and how they contribute to food addiction."

"How do you know so much about being overweight, Mrs. Laird? You're not fat."

Mrs. Laird smiled again. "I used to be addicted to food, too. I tried everything . . . diets, pills, exercise, vomiting and even laxatives. I almost died before I got help. Not until I threw away my scales and learned to accept and forgive myself, did I get myself under control. I wish those two books had been around when I was your age. They would have saved me years of misery."

Thoughtfully, Stevi looked at her watch. "Time for me to start work. Thanks for the second chance, and the tips on weight control. I promise I'll stay out of trouble."

She was almost out the door when Mrs. Laird said, "Stevi, most people can't lose on their own. I belong to a support group called Women Against Obsessive Behavior. Would you like to go with me sometime?"

"Thanks, Mrs. Laird. I'll get back to you after I read the books."

* * *

A few days later, Stevi finished reading *Overcoming Overeating*. She raced downstairs to find Mom sitting on the sofa in her housecoat reading the newspaper.

"Mom," said Stevi. "Please read this book before I return it to the library." She thrust it forward. "Then tell me what you think."

Mom flipped through it, reading excerpts here and there. She smiled, and said, "All of us overeat, don't we? Okay, I'll read it."

"Thanks, Mom." Stevi bounded back upstairs to read *It's Not What You Eat, It's What's Eating You.*

Later that week, Stevi and her mom had another conversation about weight control while fixing dinner.

"I read the book you gave me," said Mom, chopping a salad. "The concept is interesting. I'd love to throw out our scales."

"Can I try following its program? It might mean I wouldn't be eating with the family."

"You can try it, with a couple of conditions," said Mom.

Stevi set the salad on the table. "What are they?"

"You fix your own meals, then clean up after yourself. If you want any special foods that I don't buy, you pay for them."

Stevi jumped up and down. "Awesome, Mom! Thanks. You've got a deal." She danced around the kitchen while Mom laughed. "Would you like to read *It's Not What You Eat, It's What's Eating You* before I return it to the library, Mom?"

"Sure, honey," said Mom. "I'm happy you're taking better care of yourself. You're looking good. Maybe I'll try the program, too. Then I could let everybody fix their own meals." She smiled, then shook her head. "Your dad would never let us get away with that."

Stevi hugged her mother. The telephone started ringing. She raced to the hall. "I've got it."

"Hey, dude," said Mona. "You going skating this weekend with the gang?"

"Is Ari going?" Stevi crossed her fingers.

Mona giggled. "You still hot for him? I don't know if he's going. Why don't you ask him?"

Stevi's face burned. "You think he'd say yes?"

"Never know unless you ask. What's the worst that can happen. . . . He'll say no."

"I've never asked a guy for a date before."

Mona laughed. "Nothing to it. Don't be a dweeb; go for it."

"All right," said Stevi. "I will."

Chapter Seventeen

 Stevi sat cross-legged on Mona's bed, with Mona's pink princess phone in her lap, listening to Ari's telephone ring. "No answer," Stevi mouthed to Mona. She wiped one clammy hand on her jeans, and wished she had something to eat. Analyzing her desire for food, she realized she felt nervousness, not hunger. She let the phone ring a few more times, then gave up. The phone was halfway to its cradle when she heard a faint, "Hello."

"Is Ari there?"

"This is he." Ari's deep voice vibrated in her ear.

Stevi's lips moved, but no sound came out.

"Hello. *Who* is this?" Ari sounded annoyed. "Say something. I can hear you breathing."

"S-sorry, Ari, my throat was dry. How are you?"

"Stevi?"

"Yes. Hope you don't mind me calling." She hesitated. "I've never called a guy before."

Ari laughed. "Chill out, it's the nineties. What's happening?"

"I-I was wondering if you plan to go skating this weekend?"

"Are you asking me for a date?"

Stevi could hear the amusement in Ari's voice. Her heart threatened to explode. "Y-yes, I guess I am." She gripped the phone so hard her hand went numb.

"Sure, I'll go skating with you. Wear something sexy for me," his voice teased.

Stevi hung up the phone. *"Yes!"* She danced around the bedroom. "That wasn't so hard!" Giggling, she bounced on Mona's bed, then hugged her. "I can't wait until Saturday!"

Mona's eyes sparkled. "Aren't you glad you took my advice and called him! Let's get something to eat."

"Sure! I feel like I could eat a horse." Stevi stopped. "No. On second thought, just give me a diet soda. I'm not really hungry. I'm just excited."

Saturday evening, Stevi raced home from work to dress for her date with Ari. When she plunged through the door, Mom yelled from the kitchen, "Slow down, Stevi!"

Stevi bounded into the kitchen clutching an Awesome Rag's shopping bag. Mom chuckled. "What's got you so excited?"

"I'm going skating tonight with Ari. Want to see my new dress?" She ripped the bag open, then held the dress in front of her.

The cornflower-blue print fabric felt smooth against her body. The dress had a deep sweetheart neckline and a gently flaring short skirt.

Mom frowned. "The skirt's too short, and besides, you didn't ask if you could go out tonight."

Stevi stomped her foot. "Oh Mom! I'm sixteen years old, and I have my own job. Why do I need your permission to date?"

"Because you are still our child, and it's my job to know where you are, and what you're doing."

"Please don't ruin tonight for me, Mom. I've liked Ari for a long time."

"Okay," said Mom, still frowning. "But the skirt is still too short."

"So . . . I'll wear leggings."

Mom continued fixing dinner. "You're spending a lot of money on new clothes lately. I hope you're putting something into your college fund."

Stevi raced for the stairs. Over her shoulder she yelled, "Who says I'm going to college?"

Dressed, Stevi stepped back from the mirror scrutinizing her looks. The blue dress accentuated her hourglass shape; its short skirt made her silver-encased legs look long and shapely.

She pulled her shiny hair up on one side, then caught it in a glittery comb. The rest of her hair fell in soft waves. She'd shaded her eyelids with pale blue, to match her dress, and lined them with black pencil. Deep blue mascara made her golden-brown eyes look huge. She slipped on her glasses. They ruined the whole effect!

Stevi removed the glasses. She could be beautiful if she didn't have to wear them. Could she get through the evening without them? The doorbell rang.

She stuffed her glasses into a purse, grabbed her coat, then raced down the stairs and threw open the door.

Ari's black eyes glittered. He ogled her from head to toe. A whistle escaped his lips.

Stevi glowed. "Let's get out of here before my parents get nosey."

"You look awesome," said Ari, holding the car door for her.

Stevi tingled from happiness as she slipped inside.

Ari patted the seat beside him. "Don't sit over there. Come over here and be friendly."

Stevi slid across the car seat. Ari settled his arm around her shoulder, his hand falling across her breast. She shivered, then pulled slightly away so Ari's hand caressed her upper arm.

"Do you really want to go skating, Stevi?" Ari smirked. "You look *too good* to take skating."

His thumb gently stroked her upper arm, once in a while brushing the side of her breast. Stevi quivered with pleasure. "What did you have in mind?"

"I know a place where we can be alone."

She thought about what he was suggesting. "We should go skating. Everyone will be there." A tingle of danger ran through her. "Maybe we could leave early," she whispered.

Ari grinned, then started the car.

Stevi didn't do much skating. She couldn't see very well without her glasses, and Ari wanted to neck.

He pulled her toward the dark hall at the rear of the skating rink near the rest rooms. He tried to kiss her, but she coughed, then pushed him away. "I don't like it back here. There's too much cigarette smoke."

Holding her tightly, Ari stared at her cleavage. "Let's go for a ride," he said, his voice husky.

Fear, ecstasy, then confusion raced through Stevi's mind. She longed to say yes, but knew she shouldn't leave with him. *I might not get another chance.*

Finally, she decided. "Okay, but I have to tell Mona so she can cover for me in case my parents call."

Ari flashed a triumphant grin. "I'll get the car and meet you outside."

Stevi found Mona in the ladies' room. "Ari and I are going for a ride." She put her glasses on, then ran a comb through her hair.

Mona winked. "Do you have protection?"

Stevi's face reddened. She shook her head. "I don't know if I need it."

"You dweeb! Why do you think Ari wants to leave? You'd better think about what you're doing. You don't want to get pregnant or catch AIDS, do you?"

Stevi avoided Mona's eyes. "I'm not sure *what* I want," she whispered.

Mona rummaged through her purse, found what she was looking for and pressed it into Stevi's hand. "Good luck, kid."

The condom burned Stevi's hand like a hot coal. She thrust it into her bag. Thoughtfully, she stared at her reflection in the mirror. *Am I ready for sex? I look ready.* She removed her glasses, then dropped them into her purse. She wanted to look her best if she went through with it. She stepped into the night.

Chapter Eighteen

Ari opened the car door for Stevi. "Hop in, beautiful." His arm rested along the seat back; his fingers stroked her hair and the back of her neck while he drove.

Scared, Stevi huddled in the seat clinging to her purse as if it were a security blanket. Racked by indecision, she wondered how far she should go.

Ari wore a dark smile. He, too, was silent during the drive to a deserted country lane. After parking the car, he turned the radio low, then pushed the seat back as far as it would go. He pulled a half-empty bottle from the glove compartment, opened it, then offered some to Stevi.

She smelled whiskey. Shaking her head, she tried to read Ari's expression in the dark. He took a swig from the whiskey bottle. *It's as if he's done this lots of times.* Visions of Carin popped into Stevi's head. She wanted Ari to love *her.*

Everyone in the gang claimed to be having sex. But was it right for her? Was she ready?

Ari gathered Stevi in his arms. As he kissed her, the stench of whiskey assaulted her again. His kiss was demanding. He cupped her breast with one hand, tugging at the low neckline of her dress with the other. Ari's hand slid down her body to her thigh, rough skin snagging her leggings as his hand worked its way toward the hem of her dress. A wave of desire washed over Stevi.

"I love the way you feel, Stevi," muttered Ari. "You're so hot!" Ari's pupils were large with desire. His hands and kisses became more demanding.

Fear engulfed her. He was going too fast; Stevi pushed Ari away. "Please, Ari, I need to know how you feel about me."

"I want you, sweetheart." He nuzzled her hair, his lips nibbling down her neck to the top of her dress.

Stevi shoved Ari against the car seat. "NO! You've never said you love me." Tears sprang to her eyes.

"Who said anything about love? *You* asked *me* out, remember? This *is* what you wanted, isn't it?" He yanked the whiskey bottle off the dashboard, then took another long gulp.

"I want you to care about me," said Stevi. Tears drifted down her cheeks. "I need you to like me," she whispered.

"I like you." Ari leered, his eyes on Stevi's chest. "I like you a lot." He tipped the bottle to his lips, again.

In a tiny voice, Stevi said, "I don't want my first time to be like this, Ari. I'm sorry."

"What do you mean?" Ari's voice slurred. "You came *on* to me, now you want to back out?" Disgust made his face ugly.

Firmly, Stevi said, "Please take me home." Her insides quivered.

"Gnarly!" Ari growled. "I should have known . . ."

Scrunched next to the door, Stevi cried silently. Her forehead rested against the cold car window; she tasted salty tears as they ran into the corner of her mouth.

The car wheels squealed as they pulled from the gravel lane onto the highway. Ari's face was grim in the passing car headlights. The silence inside the car was as cold as a snowstorm on a midwinter day. The car stopped in front of Stevi's house.

Ari said, "You need to grow up, Stevi." When she scrambled out, he drove away.

Stevi's shoulders sagged. She scrubbed tears from her eyes, then sneaked into the dark house. Everyone was asleep. Tiptoeing into the kitchen, she found a bowl of leftover spaghetti in the refrigerator. Fork and bowl in hand, she crept to her room to comfort herself with food.

"He's disgusted with me." Tears dripped into the spaghetti. "I'm not a baby. I'm just not ready for sex." How could she have let herself get into such a situation? She paced her dark room hugging the spaghetti bowl in her arms. Toward morning, exhausted, but wide awake, she pulled a chair to her window. Resting her head on her arms, she watched the sun rise.

The great orange ball slowly peeked above the roof of a neighboring house. As the morning brightened, she noticed the backyard was beginning to green. *Spring is almost here,* she thought. Tiny leaf buds glistened as the sunlight broke through the branches of the birch tree. Nick's bike was lying in the middle of the backyard, again. "I hope it rusts," she said.

The new day gave her hope. She carried the empty spaghetti bowl through the dark house to the kitchen. *I didn't mean to binge.* She frowned. *What was it I read in* Overcoming Overeating *about bingeing?* She remembered. "Forgive yourself and move on." She began to plan. "I'll make him sorry he treated me that way. Next time, he'll ask *me* out!" She'd get her own copy of the book, then she'd ask Mrs. Laird to take her to a support group. She'd find out how much contact lenses cost and get a new hair style. Ari would notice *her.*

Chapter Nineteen

The following week, Mrs. Laird invited Stevi to a support group meeting held in her home. It was a warm evening for this time of year; the address was only a few blocks away. Stevi, dressed in new multi-colored parachute pants and blouse, decided to walk to the meeting.

Mrs. Laird led her up a short flight of steps to an L-shaped living and dining room. Stevi studied the walnut-paneled walls and shiny hardwood floors with no rugs. A contemporary sofa had gold and blue cushions. Off-white curtains with blue flecks in them covered opposite walls in each room. Bright pictures and plants brought the room to life.

Five women of varying ages and sizes sat around the room in walnut chairs. Stevi realized, uncomfortably, that she was the youngest person there.

"Girls," said Mrs. Laird. "I'd like you to meet Stevi. Stevi, starting on the right are Megan, Helen, Marg, Renie and Peggy.

We're very informal and only use first names. You can call me Donna at WAOB meetings."

Stevi sat in a chair that matched the sofa.

Donna said, "Each of us will tell you a little about herself, then you can tell us why you're here. I'll start.

"I was fat as a child. As I got older, I tried every diet or fad that came along to lose weight. Finally, I got professional help and in the process ran across the book *Overcoming Overeating*. Using its principles, this support group, and professional counseling, I've gotten my weight under control." She pointed to Megan. "Will you share next?"

Megan had curly cinnamon-red hair, big green eyes, and a squeaky voice. "Hi, Stevi. As the group knows, I've always felt deformed because of my big butt and narrow shoulders." Everyone laughed. "I became an alcoholic, but kicked alcohol by going to AA. Then, I heard about Women Against Obsessive Behavior. I liked the idea of women helping women. I've learned to like myself and I haven't had a drink in two years, *and* I haven't substituted food for alcohol."

"Would you believe I'm eighty years old?" Helen spoke softly. She looked sixty-five. "For years I tried to mold my body to what society dictated as the ideal woman. Thanks to the new trend against dieting, I've discovered that I'm not fat. I'm learning to accept the way I look after years of brainwashing."

"I wish I looked as good as Helen," said Marg, in the next chair. She was round with short graying hair, and looked to be in her mid-fifties. "My entire family is heavy. I've given up trying to fit the skinny mold. *This is the way I am!*" She grinned like a chipmunk. "I still have to work at accepting myself, or I get depressed."

"I'm Renie." Toffee-colored hair formed a frizzy ring around her head. She had a slight lisp. "I just plain like to eat. There's nothing anyone can do about me; I'll always be chubby," she said, grinning. "I come to the meetings because I like the company." Her outgoing personality twinkled in her eyes, and Stevi liked her immediately.

The last speaker was Peggy, a skinny, sullen girl only a little older than Stevi. "*They* say I'm anorexic. I'm here because my family makes me come. Personally, I think I'm fat. I hate eating and hate everyone always forcing me to eat."

"Thanks, ladies," said Donna. She handed Stevi a booklet. "We use a program based on the twelve-step program from AA. 'Food,' 'drugs' or the name of your obsessive behavior is substituted for the word 'alcohol.' You can read the steps on page two."

Stevi opened her booklet and studied the program.

"It takes a long time to work through the steps," said Donna. "While working the steps myself, I discovered I wanted to help others. Several years ago, I went back to college to train to be a counselor. One day when I get my degree, I'll go into counseling full time.

"Now, let's talk about how to feel better about yourself."

Megan said, "No more abusive remarks to yourself. What does that mean to you, Stevi?"

Stevi shrugged. "I'm not sure."

"Say, for example, you eat a couple of cookies," Megan said. "After you eat them, you feel bad because you're supposed to be on a diet. Don't tell yourself 'What's the use!' and start bingeing. Instead say, 'I needed a couple of cookies because I was upset, or bored, or tired. It's okay. I'll just start over now.' "

Stevi sat up straight. "That's what the book means by putting food in its proper place, isn't it?"

Renie smiled. "You got it, kid."

"My favorite part is staying off the scales," said Marg, laughing. "I sabotage myself when I weigh in. If my weight is down, I reward myself with food. If it's up, I get depressed and eat more. Staying off the scales and letting my clothes tell me when I'm losing helps me feel good about myself. I don't get depressed as often and I feel more in control."

"The book said to be kind to yourself," said Stevi. "I'm buying clothes that fit, and saving for contact lenses and a new hair style. Am I on the right track?"

"If all that makes you feel good," said Helen, "go for it! I'm a firm believer in being good to yourself. That's why I've lived so long."

Everyone chuckled.

The meeting lasted for two hours, then Donna served tea and coffee. "Well, Stevi, what do you think of our group?"

Stevi smiled. "I like all of you. I've never felt so comfortable in a group before. We have different problems, yet we're alike." She glanced from woman to woman. "If you'll have me, I'd like to join your group."

"Welcome to WAOB," said Megan. She gave Stevi a hug.

"Now comes the fun part," said Renie. "We stay and gossip for another couple of hours."

A few weeks later, Stevi was rummaging through her locker.

"Hey, girl friend, where you been?" Mona asked.

Stevi jumped. "You scared me. I didn't hear you coming."

Laughing, Mona clapped Stevi on the back. "You're edgy lately. How come I never see you at lunch anymore?"

"I don't eat the same time you do. I'm not hungry then, so I go for a walk," said Stevi. "I'm learning to eat only *if* I'm really hungry. I told you about the program with WAOB."

Mona stepped back for a better look. "You *are* thinner."

"Next week I get contact lenses. I've been saving for two months for them. Then I'm getting my hair cut and styled."

"I don't mean to change the subject," said Mona, "but are you going to the Spring Dance?"

Stevi stared at the floor. "No one's asked me."

"Cheer up." Mona giggled. "Ari asked me to find out if you had a date. Are you still interested in him?"

My plan's paying off. Stevi's eyes twinkled. "I still think he's to die for, but I'm not sure I should go out with him. He got drunk last time and acted like a jerk, and he hasn't apologized."

The class bell rang. "I have to get to class," Mona said and took off running down the hall. She yelled over her shoulder, "Don't be surprised to get a call from Ari soon."

Chapter Twenty

That evening the telephone rang while Stevi was dressing for work.

"Stevi?" Ari's voice caressed her ear.

She smiled, feeling powerful. *Let him sweat a little for hurting me.* "Who is this?" Her voice was sweet but cool.

"Ari," he said. Stevi didn't respond. Ari continued, "Would you like to go to the Spring Dance with me?"

"I'm not sure, Ari. I don't go out with boys who drink."

Ari cleared his throat. "I'm sorry," he muttered. "I don't drink well. It won't happen again. Forgive me?"

"*If* I forgive you, and *if* I go out with you, I want it understood there will be no fooling around. I'm not ready for sex; I only want to be friends. Before I get serious, I need to learn who I am and what I want."

"I understand," Ari said. "Does that mean you'll go out with me?"

"Yeah, I'd love to." Stevi glanced at her watch. "Got to leave for work, Ari. See you at school." Her hand still on the telephone, she stared into space. This was the first time she'd been asked to a dance this far in advance. She smiled.

The next few weeks rushed by. Stevi got contact lenses and had her hair trimmed to shoulder length in the back, with soft curls framing her face. The few new clothes she chose accented her improving figure. Proud of the way she looked, she usually had a smile for everyone as she raced between school and work.

The Spring Dance was scheduled for the second Saturday in May. Stevi and Mona planned to shop for dresses the weekend before the dance.

"Let's go to Surrell's Department Store," said Stevi.

"Surrell's is as good as anywhere," Mona mumbled, shuffling through the mall.

"I don't have much cash left after paying for my contact lenses. My parents couldn't afford to give me any extra cash this week."

"The lenses were worth it." Mona's eyes filled with envy. "You look good," she said without enthusiasm.

"Thanks," said Stevi. "I've worked hard to feel better about myself." She studied Mona's dejected figure. "Do you feel all right?"

Mona shrugged.

She and Mona searched the Fashion Dress department. "These dresses look everyday-ish to me," said Mona, listlessly. "I want to look in the Gown department." She sighed.

Concerned, Stevi asked, "Is something wrong, Mona? You aren't your normal cheerful self. You look down. You usually love shopping." They crossed the aisle to the formal gown section. The gowns glowed with sequins and glitter. Stevi checked a price tag and frowned. "I can't afford this department."

"Excuse me while I run to the ladies' room," said Mona. Stevi browsed through the gowns until Mona bounced back into the department.

"Look at the dress on this mannequin!" Mona squealed. "It's perfect for me." The simple sleeveless sheath, with a very short skirt, shimmered with gold beads. "I want to try it on. Where's a salesperson when you need one?"

Puzzled by Mona's change of attitude, Stevi said, "You go ahead and try the dress on. I'll be in Fashion Dresses where the prices are more reasonable." She abandoned Mona to the dressing room.

Back in Fashion Dresses, Stevi found a simple pink silk dress with a draped neckline. Like Mona's, it was sleeveless with an A-line skirt. This was more her speed. The dress fit perfectly. She imagined it with jewelry. Maybe Mom would let her wear the good pearls. After the dance, she could wear it to church. She double-checked the price tag. The dress cost twenty-five dollars more than she had. Her heart plunged. Sadly, she removed the dress and hung it back on the hanger.

Mona bounded over, a dress bag draped on her shoulder. "Did you find anything?"

Stevi sniffed back tears. "I found the perfect dress, but I can't afford it."

Mona extracted a credit card from her purse. "I'll give you a loan. You can pay me back next week."

Stevi threw her arms around Mona. "You're the best friend anyone ever had!" Happy tears leaked from Stevi's eyes.

On their way to her car, Mona gasped. Her hand on her chest, she choked out, "I can't breathe," then collapsed.

"Mona! What's wrong?" Stevi looked around for help. People were going in and out of the mall. "Someone call 9-1-1," she screamed.

She felt for Mona's pulse. It was faint and rapid. From the corner of her eye, she saw Mona's purse spilled open. An empty crack vile and pipe had fallen out. She remembered what she'd learned in Red Cross Emergency Training about drug overdoses, and turned Mona over so she wouldn't choke if she vomited.

A crowd gathered. Stevi felt for Mona's pulse again. "Is anyone a doctor or nurse?" She glanced at the ring of faces. A lady ran up and said the ambulance would be there in a few minutes.

A familiar voice cut through Stevi's fear. "What happened?"

Stevi looked up. Carin and Terrina crouched over her and Mona. "I think Mona used crack," said Stevi.

Carin's face got pale. "Oh no, it's my fault," she said, backing away.

"Forget that for now," said Terrina. "What can we do for Mona?"

Stevi checked her pulse again. She couldn't find it. *Mona*

wasn't breathing. "CPR! We've got to start CPR," she cried.

Terrina knelt by Stevi. "I remember it from Red Cross. Do you?"

"Yeah, let's get going." She and Terrina worked over Mona for what felt like hours until the paramedics got there.

They pushed the girls out of the way. "What happened?" one asked.

"We think she used crack," said Stevi, glancing at Terrina for confirmation.

He slipped an oxygen mask over Mona's face. Working over her, one paramedic said, "We've got a pulse. Let's get her to the hospital."

Terrina said, "Stevi, go with her. Carin and I will get your packages and meet you there."

Stevi called her mom from the hospital. Mom asked, "Did someone call Mona's parents?"

"I think so," said Stevi. She was shaking, now that the crisis was over.

"Do you want us to come be with you?"

"Terrina and Carin are here," said Stevi. "I'll call you if I need you. Thanks, Mom."

Stevi returned to the waiting room. Carin huddled in the corner crying and muttering to herself, while Terrina paced.

Suddenly, Mona's parents rushed in. "What happened?" Mrs. Webb screamed. "Where's my baby?"

Mr. Webb put his arm around his wife. "Calm down, honey." Turning to Stevi he asked, "Have you gotten any word yet? Can you tell us what happened?"

Carin wailed, "It's all my fault. I gave it to her. I'm so sorry. I never thought anyone would get hurt. I'll never do drugs again." She buried her face in her hands.

Stevi hugged Mrs. Webb, then told Mona's parents what had happened. "I'm praying for her," she said.

Finally, the doctor came into the waiting room. "She'll be all right," he said. "She was lucky she was with friends who knew how to help her. A lot of crack overdoses don't make it."

"Thank God," said Stevi, beginning to cry.

Mona's mom burst into tears. "Thank you," she sobbed.

To Stevi she said, "Mona might have died if you hadn't been with her. How can we ever repay you?"

Two evenings later, Stevi told her support group what had happened. Donna said, "Would you like to invite your friends to join us? While we don't counsel drug addicts specifically, we could help your friends by letting them talk about their problems. Then maybe they wouldn't feel the need for drugs."

"That would be wonderful," said Stevi. "I'm worried that there is a real drug problem in school. Drugs are so easy to buy. Still, you'd think that with all the information on TV about the dangers of drug use, kids would think twice before trying them."

"Is there a drug counseling program at your school? If not," said Donna, "I can help you get one set up. I know several people from college who specialize in drug counseling."

"What an awesome idea. We could start support groups for teenagers," said Stevi. "I've even thought of a name. How about TNT—Teens Nurturing Teens?"

Chapter Twenty-one

 Friday, a new girl entered gym class, her fat stomach jiggling like jelly. Stevi heard some guys from the boys' class making jokes about her. While Mrs. Nolan got volley-ball equipment out, Stevi remembered her first day of the school year. She marched over to the new girl. "Hi, my name's Stevi. I haven't seen you before."

The girl hung her head; stringy clay-colored hair fell in her face. "I just moved here," she whispered. "My name's Janee."

"Glad to meet you, Janee. Hope we can be friends. Will you sit with me at lunch?"

Janee peeked at Stevi. "I'd love to." Her smile lit up her face. "Thanks for being nice to me; most kids aren't." She looked away. "Especially popular ones like you," she whispered.

"Me, popular?" Stevi laughed. "You must be kidding."

Timidly, Janee said, "You're so pretty. I saw on a poster that you've been nominated for the Spring Queen."

"I don't expect to win." Stevi shrugged. "At lunch I'll tell you a story. I was heavy at the beginning of the school year. I'd love to tell you about how I changed."

Hope shone in Janee's green eyes.

After lunch, Stevi studied her homework while waiting for math class to begin. The room suddenly became quiet. Glancing up, she spotted Mona, in school for the first time since the drug over-dose.

Mona hesitated in the doorway, pale and looking scared.

Stevi smiled and waved toward the desk next to her. "Welcome back, Mona."

Tension in the room dissolved. Gratitude shining from her eyes, Mona hugged Stevi. "Thanks, girl friend. You don't know how hard it is to walk into a room after making a fool of yourself like I did. I'm just glad it happened on a weekend and not in school. I could have been expelled."

"How did you get hooked on drugs like that, Mona? I knew you tried them when we went horseback riding," said Stevi. "But I didn't realize you continued taking them."

Mona hung her head. "At first they make you feel so wonder-ful. Then, when you come down you feel rotten and think one more time won't be a problem. Before you realize what's happened, you have a habit you can't control." Her gaze swept over their class-mates, then returned to Stevi. "By the way, I haven't thanked you for saving my life."

"Terrina helped," said Stevi. "I'm just glad the school offered the Red Cross Emergency Training Course last fall." Stevi twisted a pencil in her fingers, then peeked at Mona. "Are you off the drugs now?"

Tears welled up in Mona's eyes. "I want them all the time, but yes . . . I'm off them. I'm seeing a drug counselor at the hospital several times a week. I have a long way to go. Will you help me?"

Stevi stared into Mona's troubled eyes, then smiled. "Of course I will. That's what friends are for! Besides, I owe you for helping me get my weight under control, don't I?"

The evening of the dance a light rain was falling. The night was warm with a soft breeze. The weatherman had promised the rain would end early. At seven-thirty the doorbell rang and Nick ran to answer it. "Hi, Ari. Come to pick up the blimp?"

"Nick, don't talk about your sister that way," said Dad from the living room.

Red-faced, Ari stumbled into the house, carrying a small florist's box. "Is Stevi ready?"

"STEVI, YOUR DATE'S HERE!" Nick yelled.

Stevi, watching from the stairs, ran back to her room and gave herself one last glance in the mirror. Her pink dress fit perfectly. Mom's pearls glistened around her neck, and her eyes, without glasses, sparkled like obsidian. She descended the stairs slowly.

Ari's eyes widened. "WOW!" he said. "You're beautiful!"

Stevi grinned, blinking her eyelashes at him. "Thank you." She spied the box. "Is that for me?"

She removed a spray of tiny pink roses from the clear plastic box, breathed in their fragrance, and handed them back to Ari to slip onto her wrist.

Ari, a perfect gentleman the whole way to the dance, dropped Stevi off at the school's front door. "Hurry inside," he said. "I don't want my date getting wet."

Stevi ran up the steps. Someone flung the door open, and she dashed inside. Loud music blared from the gym. She peeked inside the doors. The gym was decorated with pink and yellow streamers. Refreshment tables were set up across the far wall, with a group of folding chairs nearby. Bunches of pink and yellow paper flowers brightened the tables.

Soon Ari's arm slipped around Stevi's waist. "Ready to party?" He guided her across the crowded dance floor toward the refreshment table where Jake and Mona were arguing. "What's going on?"

Jake opened his jacket. A bottle of whiskey snuggled inside his pocket. "I thought I'd liven up the punch."

Ari shook his head. "The bottle's too small, Jake. We'd be better off only spiking our drinks."

"You said you wouldn't drink," said Stevi.

"Especially if you're driving," said Mona.

Jake pointed at Stevi. "*You* be our designated driver, Stevi."

"I don't have my license yet," she said. "My parents said I have to wait until I'm seventeen."

"I'll drive tonight," said Ari. "I don't need alcohol to have fun with Stevi."

Stevi gave a silent prayer of thanks.

The band started playing a slow song. Ari pulled Stevi into his arms. "I *promised* I wouldn't drink," he whispered holding her closely. They danced as if they'd practiced together for years.

When the music stopped, Ari excused himself to go to the rest room. Stevi weaved her way through the dancers looking for a chair. Halfway across the room, Brian caught her arm. "Will you dance with me, Stevi?"

"Sure!" She and Brian began to writhe to the wild music. The song ended and the music flowed directly into a slow dance. Brian pulled Stevi into his arms. "You look awesome tonight. I hope you'll dance with me later."

As Brian whirled her around, Stevi noticed Ari standing on the sidelines, scowling. She grinned and waved. "I came with Ari, Brian. After this dance, I have to spend some time with him."

Brian stared deep into Stevi's eyes. "Would you consider going out with me?" Stunned, Stevi didn't answer.

Ari strolled over. "May I have my date back?"

Brian winked at Stevi. "Remember your promise?"

"What's he talking about?" Ari's manner was stiff.

Stevi grinned. "He wants another dance later."

The music started again. She and Ari danced until Jesse cut in. "Want to dance, Stevi?"

Ari looked angry. "It's up to her." He glared at Stevi, then stalked away.

"Okay, Jesse." Happily, Stevi slipped into his arms. He was so tall. She felt tiny next to him.

Ari claimed the next three dances. "I've never had so much fun at a dance," said Stevi. "I'm usually a wallflower."

"You're a wonderful dancer, Stevi," said Ari. "Let's go outside for some air. It's stopped raining and the moon is out."

Outside, Ari complained, "Do you have to dance with every guy in school?"

Stevi laughed. "I'm only dancing with our friends. You don't *own* me, and *you* can dance with anyone you want."

"I'd like to own you," he said, frowning. "Will you go steady with me?"

"We talked about this, Ari. I'm too young to get serious. For the first time in my life, I have lots of friends and I want to be free; but I really like you. You'll always be special to me."

"I messed up last time we dated, didn't I?"

"No, we *both* did, but let's always be friends." Stevi snuggled her head against Ari's shoulder.

Mona bounded down the steps. "There you are! Come back inside. It's time to announce the queen."

The school principal, Mr. Rogers, was standing on a raised platform. "It's time to vote for the Spring Queen. While the band plays, fill out your ballot and vote for Mona Webb, Terrina Jones or Stevi Power. Drop your ballot cards into the box near the refreshment table. Mrs. Nolan and I will count the votes after this song is finished, and then we'll crown the new Spring Queen." While the band started playing, several senior boys pushed a chair draped with red velvet from behind a curtain to act as a throne.

A girl Stevi didn't know handed out the ballots. Stevi giggled, then whispered into Ari's ear. "You *are* voting for me, aren't you?"

Ari feigned surprise. "No!" He laughed. "I'm voting for Terrina." When Stevi pretended to be hurt, Ari said, "Of course I'm voting for you."

They circled their choices and then dropped the ballots into the ballot box. Ari led Stevi to the dance floor. When the band played a second song, Jake cut in. He said, "Mona better watch out. You're getting so foxy, she's got real competition."

Stevi shook her head. "Mona doesn't need to worry. She's in a class all her own."

The bandleader announced a break. Mr. Rogers clapped his hands for silence. "The big moment is here," he said. Mrs. Nolan handed him an envelope. He fumbled for his glasses, creating suspense.

Stevi's heart swelled with pride. *Imagine having been nominated.* She remembered the first day of school when she was embarrassed by ripping the seams out of her gym suit. *I've come a long way.*

"The winner is . . ." said Mr. Rogers, glancing at each girl in turn, "Mona Webb."

Mona squealed, and threw her arms around Jake. Her eyes sparkled. Jake escorted Mona to the stage where Mr. Rogers placed a crown of flowers on Mona's head, then stepped back clapping. Mrs. Nolan handed her a bouquet of yellow roses.

Stevi ran to Mona and threw her arms around her friend. "Congratulations! I'm happy you won."

Mona hugged back—hard. "I have *you* to thank. I almost blew it by taking the drugs. I wish we both could win."

"I never expected to win. It was awesome just to be nominated." Stevi winked. "But watch out next year, girl friend. I'll beat the jeans off you!" She laughed, then hugged her friend again.

Bibliography

BOOKS

Atkins, Robert C. *Dr. Atkins' New Diet Revolution.* New York: M. Evans and Company, Inc., 1992.

Atrens, Dale M. *Don't Diet.* New York: William Morrow and Company, Inc., 1988.

Baumann, Tyeis Baker and McFarland, Barbara. *Feeding the Empty Heart.* San Francisco: Harper & Row Publishers, 1988.

Berger, Gilda. *Crack, the New Drug Epidemic!* New York: Franklin Watts, 1987.

Chomet, Julian. *Understanding Drugs (Cocaine and Crack).* New York: Franklin Watts, 1987.

Eades, Michael R. *Thin So Fast.* New York: Warner Books, 1989.

Edelstein, Barbara. *The Woman Doctor's Diet for Teen-Age Girls.* Englewood Cliffs, NJ: Prentice-Hall, Inc., 1980.

Gardner, Joseph L., ed. *Eat Better, Live Better.* Pleasantville, NY: The Reader's Digest Association, Inc., 1982.

Greeson, Janet. *It's Not What You're Eating, It's What's Eating You.* New York: Pocket Books, 1990.

Hirschmann, Jane R. and Munter, Carol H. *Overcoming Overeating.* Reading, MA: Addison-Wesley Publishing Company, Inc., 1988.

Johanson, Chris-Ellyn. *Encyclopedia of Psychoactive Drugs (Cocaine, a New Epidemic).* New York: Chelsea House Publishers, 1986.

Katahn, Martin. *The Rotation Diet.* New York: W. W. Norton & Company, 1986.

LeShan, Eda J. *Winning the Losing Battle.* New York: Crowell, 1979.

Sandbek, Terence J. *The Deadly Diet: Recovering from Anorexia and Bulimia.* Oakland, CA: New Harbinger Publications, 1986.

NEWSPAPERS

Chaplin, A. M. "Rethinking Thin," *Sunday Magazine,* Baltimore Sun Papers, June 2, 1991.

PERIODICALS

Reader's Digest (listed in order of date)
　Carper, Jean. "Everyday Foods That Fight Cholesterol," December 1988.
　Green, Lee. "Hidden Fats: Key to Weight Control," February 1989.
　McConnell, Malcolm. "Crack Invades the Countryside," February 1989.
　Englebardt, Stanley L. "Are You Over-Exercising?" March 1989.
　Katahn, Martin. "Diet the T-Factor Way," October 1989.
　Giller, Robert M. and Matthews, Kathy. "Rev Up, Lose Weight, Feel Great!" March 1990.
　(Consumer Reports). "Are You Eating Wisely?" September 1990.
　Colvin, Robert H. and Olson, Susan C. "The Last Diet You'll Ever Need," March 1991.
　Antonello, Jean. "Get Thin, Stay Thin," May 1991.
　Long, Patricia, "Shortcuts to a Low-Fat Diet," August 1991.
　Fletcher, Anne M. "Thin For Life," September 1991.
　Skalka, Patricia. "Snack Your Way to Great Shape," November 1991.
　Castleman, Michael. "You Can Lose Those Holiday Pounds," January 1992.
　Hales, Dianne. "Eat Smart, Feel Good, Look Great," February 1992.
　Benson, Herbert, Stuart, Eileen M., and Associates of the Mind/Body Medical Institute. "Think Yourself Thin," March 1992.